LAURA
POSSESSED

LAURA
POSSESSED

A Novel of Suspense

ANTHEA FRASER

Dodd, Mead & Company · New York

ISBN: 0-396-06975-4
Library of Congress Catalog Card Number: 74-3785
Printed in the United States of America
by Vail-Ballou Press, Inc., Binghamton, N.Y.

Contents

PART 1

Laura

Chapter 1

·I T   W A S   ironic that it should have been the ordinariness of the village that first struck her—ironic in view of the fact that she was later to consider it a landscape of the damned.

Edward had collected her from Richard's flat soon after lunch and this was the first afternoon since leaving hospital that she had not retired to bed. "Rest, rest, and more rest," Dr. Banstead had emphasized when at last he relinquished his charge of her. "The headaches will go in time, but don't despair if it takes longer than you'd hoped. Remember your nervous system is having to recover not only from your own injuries in the crash but from the shock of your mother's death as well. When you get to your brother's, see the local doctor and give him this note, which will put him in the picture." Fleetingly, Laura wondered what he had written.

Neither Richard nor his current girl friend had been at the flat to hand her formally into Edward's care, and though Laura herself had perfectly understood the reasons for their absence, Edward was distinctly annoyed.

"If this is the way they've been looking after you for the last two weeks, it's just as well you're coming back with me now," he remarked tightly as he helped her into the car.

"They did explain, Edward," she murmured in their defence. "It's just that this is a particularly important rehearsal—the producer wants to change the wording in one

3

scene and Richard is determined not to let him get away with it. He has to be there, and Gillian, of course, is playing the lead."

"It's high time he settled down and married," retorted Edward, unmollified. "He's thirty-three now but he still persists in living the same Bohemian existence he embarked on at University. Young Toby has far more sense of responsibility."

"Well, after all, he's married."

"Precisely, and so should Richard be. Honestly, Laura, if it weren't for his string of girls, I'd begin to have serious doubts about him!"

She gave a little spurt of laughter. "I'm quite sure you needn't! And there's no need to worry on my behalf either—they've been perfectly sweet to me, even though that flat puts rather a strain on a *ménage à trois*."

Edward didn't reply and she snuggled down into the collar of her coat. Truth to tell, she would much rather have stayed on with Richard and Gillian in their London flat than set off for this remote Kent village to make her home with Edward and Caroline, kind though they had been to insist on it. At least, Edward had insisted. Laura doubted if Caroline was too pleased. There had always been a certain restraint between her and her sister-in-law.

They drove in silence for some time, threading their way through the depressing outskirts of London into the first, tentative greenness of Kent. Laura found her eyelids drooping, and as her consciousness released its hold, her mind fluttered feebly back over the last horrifying months—the trauma of the crash itself and its attendant bereavement, the desolate days spent lying in the hospital bed.

Beside her, Edward cleared his throat and her eyes

flickered open. Despite his long silence, he had apparently continued to brood on his brother's shortcomings.

"Ideally, of course, you should have come to us straight from hospital, but to start with, the doctors thought a long car journey at that stage would tire you, and then, with its being the school holidays at the time, Four Winds would hardly have been restful for you anyway."

" 'Four Winds,' " Laura repeated slowly, and shivered a little. "It sounds a lonely, desolate kind of place!"

He laughed. "Neither lonely nor desolate, I assure you. Merely a comfortable house standing at the crossroads above the village. Strange to think you've never seen it."

"How long is it since you moved in?"

"Almost three months now. We're quite at home."

"You've never regretted moving so far out of town?" Laura enquired, remembering her own and her mother's surprise at Edward and Caroline's plumping for village life.

"Not in the slightest. After all, I don't have to come to London often and Brocklehurst is very convenient for the paper—I can be at my desk twenty minutes after leaving home."

"I could never understand why you left the Ledbrook house, though. You could have been at your desk in ten minutes from there!"

"Well, Caroline never cared for it all that much, and when they started some new development just opposite, she couldn't wait to get away." He smiled a little. "I think, bless her heart, she rather fancies herself as lady of the manor up at Four Winds."

"I should have thought she'd be bored in the country. After all, Ledbrook is a busy little market town with plenty going on, her precious bridge club, the cinema—"

"Not to mention a thriving newspaper!" put in Edward.

"As you say! But from what I hear, Brocklehurst sounds at the back of beyond."

"Well, Caroline seems to find plenty to do. She's hardly ever at home. But I am a little worried that you might be bored, at least until you're well enough to find yourself another job. You'll obviously have to spend a fair portion of your time resting for the next month or two, and if you could find some absorbing hobby to bury yourself in, so much the better. In fact, it's the perfect chance for you to take up writing again."

Laura smiled. " 'The Literary Hardys.' I have rather fallen by the wayside in that respect, haven't I? But the rest of you are keeping the flag flying—you as editor of the *Ledbrook Courier*, Richard with his avant-garde television plays, and Toby as art critic churning out his volumes of poetry on the side."

"That's as may be, but you're still the only one to have followed in Father's footsteps with a novel. How old were you when it came out—seventeen? We were all set to have a literary genius on our hands, but you've never attempted anything since, have you?"

"No, it was probably just a flash in the pan, to prove to myself that I could do it."

"Don't you think it's about time for another flash?"

"It's a thought, certainly, while I'm stuck in the house, but I don't know that I could do it again. My powers of concentration are a bit erratic at the moment, and, anyway, Royalists and Roundheads don't inspire me any more."

"It needn't be historical this time. You could try your hand at something entirely new. Anyway, think about it. And here we are now on the outskirts of Brocklehurst."

6

Laura sat up eagerly and was immediately aware of a sense of disappointment. She had hoped at least for her exile to be spent in a picturesque village, with perhaps the occasional oasthouse to add a touch of interest to the skyline. But from what she could see, Brocklehurst certainly couldn't be considered pretty or even interesting. In fact, its unimaginative houses were reminiscent of a child's drawing, each set squarely in a postage-stamp garden so that they lined the road solidly like a row of dumpy, middle-aged matrons.

Admittedly there was the usual village green, where doubtless local cricket matches were played on summer weekends, but at the moment its very greenness, dull and unrelieved, merely intensified the drabness. All in all, it was so uninspired, so conventional, that it bored her at the first glance and she moved restlessly with the impatience of the invalid.

Edward glanced sideways at her. "Tired? We're nearly home now."

They drove down the long winding street past a squat, uninteresting church. Once beyond the cluster of shops the road began to climb, and minutes later, Edward turned left between some high, wrought-iron gates. They had arrived.

Laura looked up at the house in front of them and pulled her coat more tightly about her, reluctant now to leave the secluded warmth of the car and go out into her new life, but Edward had already slammed his door and come round to help her out.

"A cup of tea wouldn't go amiss, would it?" he said rallyingly, taking her arm and leading her up the three shallow steps. "Then I think it would be an idea for you to have a rest until dinner." He leant forward and opened the front door. "Caroline! We're here!"

Ahead of them lay a large, pleasant hall, bright and welcoming, but without warning a sudden, choking feeling of terror rushed over her and she pulled violently back against the pressure of Edward's arm. In that instant she was overpoweringly aware of an almost tangible wave of despair emanating from the house, making her gasp as its cold desolation flooded over her.

Frantically she tried to fight off Edward's tightening grip, with some half-formed panic idea of turning and running, running anywhere, just as long as she need never take that fateful step over the threshold.

"Laura! For God's sake, what's the matter? It's all right—we're home now!"

Her brief spurt of energy, born of desperation, subsided as abruptly as it had come and she went limp, falling against Edward as he half-carried her into the hall. He lowered her gently onto a carved monk's bench which stood against the wall and stood staring down at her.

"What the hell was all that about? You're as white as a sheet!"

It was already too late. She had entered the house, albeit against her will, and now the inescapable consequences would follow. It had been foolish to think she could resist them.

"Laura!"

Dazedly she looked up, her eyes focussing on Edward's anxious face, and she gave herself a little shake. Her tongue, stiff and awkward, moved over her parched lips. "I'm sorry, Edward, it was just—just the change of temperature, I suppose." She shivered violently and added, almost inaudibly, "It's so *cold!*"

"Cold? Good Lord, girl, Caroline keeps this place like a

8

hothouse!" His voice softened. "It's because you're weak and tired that you feel chilly. Knowing Caro, there'll be a fire in the sitting-room anyway, even though the central heating boiler's going full belt. Come on, I'll help you in there." He raised his voice. "Caroline! Where are you?"

A voice from upstairs called back, "Coming!" and a moment later, as Edward helped Laura into a comfortable chair by the sitting-room fire, Caroline hurried into the room.

"Sorry, I didn't hear you arrive. Welcome to Four Winds, Laura!" She broke off, glancing apprehensively at the beads of perspiration on her sister-in-law's white face. "Is she all right?" she asked doubtfully.

Edward straightened. "I don't know. I had the devil of a job to get her through the front door."

"Through——?"

"I'm all right, Caroline," Laura put in quietly. "I'm just—cold—that's all."

"You'll soon warm up in here. Mrs. Baines is bringing in some tea and there's hot buttered toast too."

There was a pause while they both stood looking down at her and, feeling something was required of her, Laura said dutifully, "This is a pretty room."

Her everyday comment had the desired effect and they both relaxed, Edward to remove his overcoat and Caroline to bend to the cigarette box on the coffee table.

"Yes, we're rather pleased with the effect. In fact, we're delighted with the whole house. When you've had a rest, I'll show you over it." She smiled. "It's abnormally tidy at the moment, now that Robert and Helen have gone back to school, but Peter will soon put an end to that. He makes more mess than the other two put together!"

"Where's Peter now?" Laura felt as though she were

memorizing a script, hoping that the right words would follow on the right cues, but Caroline seemed unaware of her stiffness.

"He doesn't get back from school till almost six. We have a rota, three other mothers and I. It's my turn next week to do the car-run. Ah, here's tea. Mrs. Baines, this is my sister-in-law, Miss Hardy."

Laura nodded at the pleasant-looking woman who set the silver tray down carefully on the low table. The teapot and hot water jug glinted like molten copper in the firelight.

Caroline handed her a fragile cup and saucer and lifted the lid off the toast dish. "Take two—they're minute."

Obediently Laura lifted the tiny, butter-impregnated triangles of glistening toast.

"And how's brother Richard? Still surrounded by a host of adoring women?"

"Only one at a time," Laura answered quietly. She always felt this need with both her married brothers and their disapproving wives to defend charming, unconventional Richard.

Caroline gave a short laugh. "I suppose that's something! What's the current one like?"

"Perfectly sweet—you've probably seen her on TV—Gillian Marlowe. She was in the Herries series."

"The redhead? Yes, I know the one. And what about Toby and Janet? Any news of them?"

"They came to see me in hospital, of course, but they couldn't stay long because of the baby. Haven't you seen them for a while?"

"No, but no doubt I shall now, and Richard too. You'll draw them like bees to a honeypot." Her voice, despite its lightness, had a slight edge to it. Laura was well aware that a lot of Caroline's resentment of her stemmed from the obvious devotion of her three elder brothers. "Never mind, one advantage—if it can be called that—of a house this size is that there's enough room to accommodate all one's relations when they suddenly decide that they can't possibly manage a week longer without spending a couple of days with you. Which is what will happen, mark my words!"

Laura said deprecatingly, "They really kept in touch with me because of Mother." Her voice trembled and Caroline, instantly ashamed, bent forward and took her hand.

"Try not to think about it if you can."

"But I saw her, Caroline," Laura said unsteadily. "I saw her die. How can I forget that?"

"Of course you can't forget it, but if you try to close your mind to it, it will gradually get easier. At the moment the most important thing is to get you completely well again."

Edward, who had rather pointedly taken his cup of tea across to the window away from the heat of the fire, spoke for the first time.

"I was suggesting Laura might try her hand at writing again. It would help to pass the time until she can get out and about."

"That's a wonderful idea! We've a good little mobile library which comes twice a week if you need reference books, or I could always get them for you in Ledbrook."

Laura laughed protestingly. "Don't rush me. I haven't really thought about it yet, but in any case it wouldn't be historical this time, I think. In fact—" She paused, a slight frown creasing her brow.

"What?"

11

"It just occurred to me that if I did attempt something, I'd rather like to write about—about violence in the world today." She stopped abruptly and gave an uncertain laugh. "Heaven knows why; it just suddenly came into my head!"

"Sounds rather sinister!" Caroline said with a delicate shiver.

"Yes, but fascinating. What's the reason for it all? Why, suddenly, do we have these outbursts of assassinations, hijackings, kidnappings—"

"Because," put in Edward drily, "we haven't had a war for thirty years and man is naturally an aggressive animal."

"Spoken like an Englishman, darling!" Caroline remarked. "What do you imagine has been going on in Korea, Vietnam, Palestine—even Ireland, over the last twenty years? No war, indeed!"

"No major war, I meant. Only limited numbers were involved and the rest of us have to suppress our aggression as best we can. In some cases that causes trouble. Remember me speaking of Clive Sandilands, Laura? You should have a word with him. He's engaged in writing a book on America in the sixties to be called, I believe, *The Violent Decade*. He could well be of some help to you."

"I don't know that I'd dare to approach anyone as eminent as Clive Sandilands," Laura murmured, "even if he is a friend of yours."

"As a matter of fact, you'll have the chance to meet him on Sunday. Tom Howard, the managing director of our newspaper group, is giving a cocktail party. We're all invited and I know for a fact that Clive will be there. He's only over here for a couple of weeks—virtually lives in the States now. If you're really interested in violence, he's the one to fill you in."

12

"I very much doubt whether I'll be up to a cocktail party," Laura said dubiously. At last the heat from the fire was beginning to soothe away the deep chill that had enveloped her, and her eyelids felt heavy again.

Caroline reached forward and took her empty cup. "I thought you'd be tired and when I heard Edward call, I slipped into your room and switched on the electric blanket. It will be nice and warm for you now."

"That sounds very tempting."

"Edward, have you brought the cases in from the car? Perhaps you could get them while I take Laura up."

Laura allowed herself to be helped to her feet, dismayed at her extreme lassitude. Her footsteps faltered as they reached the hall and she glanced almost fearfully towards the front door. It looked perfectly ordinary—a solid, handsome oak door with nothing about it to account for those few moments of paralyzing terror. Yet even as she reassured herself, she was aware of a movement just beyond her vision and turned quickly, expecting that someone else had come into the hall. There was no one there, but the remembered sense of creeping cold stole back towards her.

"All right?" Caroline asked, feeling her involuntary jerk. Her breath was shallow and uneven and she had none to spare for a reply. She nodded and went on up the stairs, Caroline's arm supporting her.

The bedroom into which they went was bright and fresh with a pretty floral paper and pale blue carpet. A gas-fire boosted the heat from the radiator which ran under the window, and Laura exclaimed with pleasure. Pushing aside her uneasiness, she moved across to the window and leant for a moment on the sill looking out across the garden.

"What strange, twisted trees!" she commented. "I bet the boys have a marvellous time climbing them!"

"Trees?" Caroline paused in the act of turning down the counterpane. "What trees?"

"Those, at the bottom of the garden." Laura turned back to the window and stiffened unbelievingly. Beyond the lawn and flower beds was a neat patch of soil obviously destined later in the year to supply the vegetables for the house.

"But—I'm sure I saw—"

"You mean the pear and the plum, against the wall?"

"No, I—they were down at the bottom—"

"Possibly in the first quick glance your mind transposed them. I've often done that myself when I'm tired. Come on now, slip off your dress and get under the covers. Shall I help you?"

"No, I can manage, thank you. And, Caroline—"

"Yes?"

"I do appreciate it, you and Edward having me here."

"It's the least we could do," Caroline said briskly. "Lie down now and rest and I'll give you a call half an hour before dinner. Sleep well." She left the room, closing the door behind her.

Laura stood in the middle of the floor and drew a deep, quivering breath. In spite of what Caroline had said about transposing the image of the fruit trees, she was not convinced. It was not fruit trees she had seen down there against the far wall of the garden but dark, oddly twisted trees huddled close together like a crowd of small, crippled old men. She shuddered and, unbuttoning her dress, stepped out of it and laid it over the chair, but instead of getting straight into bed, she crouched down on the rug by the gas-fire, welcoming its warm rays on her thin bare arms. The last hour had been quite traumatic. She tried to

14

fight down the memory of the sensation she had experienced as she entered the house, and yet it was impossible to blot out completely because, to a lesser extent, it was here in the room with her now, an undeniable sense of desperate, hopeless waiting. Once again she thought she caught the flicker of movement out of the corner of her eye, again she turned her head sharply, though this time she knew there could be no one there.

She was not aware how long she stayed crouched on the rug in her petticoat, but at last, unsteadily, she made her way over to the bed and gratefully inched between the warm sheets, drawing them up over her shoulders. She had forgotten to turn off the gas-fire and it popped and hissed gently against the far wall, but she was too warm and drowsy to get out of bed.

So here she was, at Four Winds. Once again the little tremor ran down her spine as it had each time she heard the name of this house, ever since Edward had bought it months ago. Everything is all right, she told herself confusedly. She was in a warm, comfortable room, surrounded by normal people doing everyday things. If she strained her ears, she could hear Mrs. Baines moving about in the kitchen below. Edward and Caroline would be in the pleasant sitting-room she had just left, and soon nine-year-old Peter would be home from school. How, in the midst of all this happy bustle, could she—and apparently only she—be aware of this strange undercurrent, this pervading sense of tragedy? And whether that tragedy lay in the past or the future, or whether it straddled them both, there was no way of knowing.

Then, from one instant to the next, she must have slept, for she was in another room that she had never seen before, and there was a man with her, a man who held and kissed her with increasing urgency while she clung to him with eyes open so as to miss no moment of his closeness. He moved his head away slightly to look down at her and every feature of his face imprinted itself on her mind in her frenzied desire to memorize each detail, as though she knew that inevitably they must soon part.

It was an attractive, though self-indulgent face with heavily lidded eyes of a slaty grey-blue, a broad nose and full, sensual mouth. His chin had a slight cleft in it and his dark hair, shaggy and overlong, fell forward over his broad forehead. Smilingly he endured her intense scrutiny. He lifted a hand and almost reverently touched her face.

"I worship you, Noel," he said softly. "Do you know that?"

Slowly, as her eyes strained towards him, his features began to blur and fade and she cried out with a sense of unbearable loss. She could hear her own voice clearly and then, still in the coils of the dream, Caroline's: "Laura! Are you all right?"

"Laura"? The name was frighteningly unfamiliar. Frantically she struggled awake, half of her trying to delve back into the dream, the other half desperately seeking to escape from it.

Caroline stood by the bed looking down at her. "I heard you call out. You must have been dreaming. In any case I was just coming—it's almost seven. We usually eat at seven-thirty, but there's time for a bath first if you'd like one. The bathroom's next door."

She switched the light on as she went out. For a long moment Laura lay still. Then, as the trembling abated, she swung her legs to the floor and reached for her dressing-gown.

Chapter 2

DURING the next few days, Laura despairingly tried to stamp down her growing awareness of that strange force which seemed to follow her about the house. Brought up in a rational household, she was convinced that this awareness, obviously peculiar to herself, must be brought about by some malfunction of her brain as a result of the car crash. Far, far better to endure those searing, iron-banded headaches than this delusion. Nor dare she confide her uneasiness to Edward or Caroline, in case they should feel she was not after all well enough to be out of hospital.

Unfortunately, Caroline's insistence on plenty of rest meant that she had to spend long hours alone in her bedroom, and after the pleasant normality of lunch, it was with a sense of dread that Laura had to steel herself to go upstairs, knowing that "she" would be waiting. Caroline had brushed aside her timid suggestion that she could rest equally well on the sitting-room sofa by declaring that if she were downstairs, she was sure to be disturbed by the general bustle of the household. Laura found herself wondering a little uncharitably whether part of the reason was that Caroline preferred to have her out of the way for most of the afternoon.

The dream she had had that first afternoon occupied Laura's mind continually that week. She recalled it with distaste and embarrassment, and her memory of the man's face, as clear in her mind as when she had dreamt it, awoke in her a feeling of acute dislike rather than the passion of her dream.

Over lunch one day, she questioned Caroline about the history of the house, wondering if anything in its past might explain her present discomfort.

"Funnily enough," Caroline told her, "it used to belong to the family of a man Edward knows. Apparently he spent his childhood here, before and during the war. I don't know what happened after that. He became a journalist, which is how Edward met him, and travelled freelance all over the world."

"And presumably while he was away his family moved?"

"I suppose so. But he must feel his roots are here. He came back to this country a few months ago and is now thinking of buying a house in the district."

"Have you met him?"

"Yes." Some indefinable note in her voice made Laura glance at her, but she went on quickly, "I told him he must come to dinner one evening and see Four Winds as it is today."

"I imagine it'll be very different from how he knew it."

"Lord, yes. It had been empty for some time when Edward and I found it—broken panes and flaking brown paint—you know the kind of thing. We had workmen in the house for three solid months—central heating engineers, plumbers, plasterers, electricians—you name them, we had them!"

None of which, concluded Laura ruefully, threw the least light on what was troubling her.

She did not really want to go to the cocktail party that Sunday, but Edward would take no refusal.

"I'll make sure you don't get too tired and we shan't stay

long, and it will do you good to see some new faces. We can't have you turning into a recluse! You do seem to have been rather nervous the last few days. A change of scene will make all the difference. Anyway, I want you to meet Clive Sandilands and collect some facts about violence."

Laura smiled. "You're determined I should write that book, aren't you?"

"*A* book, yes. The choice of subject matter was yours, and I must admit it surprised me rather."

"It surprised me too," Laura said frankly. "I hadn't realized I was sufficiently interested in the subject. I always skip the more lurid descriptions in the papers. Perhaps it stems from my own accident—a personality change!" She was smiling but watched his face closely to see whether he reacted to the suggestion.

"Jekyll and Hyde? Not quite your thing, sweetie."

"But *could* it all have a lasting effect, Edward?" Laura persisted in a low voice, anxious, now that the subject had been broached, to probe a little deeper.

"The crash? I shouldn't think so. It would have manifested itself before this, anyway."

And with that she had to be content. Perhaps he was right, she thought as she prepared for the party, and all she needed was to be taken out of herself. But as the everyday expression passed through her mind, it jolted to a startled standstill. "To be taken out of herself"—what an annihilating thought! She caught up her handbag and went running out of the room and down the stairs to where Edward stood waiting.

Afterwards, when the choking, dizzy panic had receded slightly, Laura was convinced that she had known as she went into Tom Howard's house what she would find there, and it was with a sense of blind fatalism that she

19

looked across the room full of people to see the man from her dream standing by the fireplace. It couldn't be happening, but it was. She was seized with a fit of uncontrollable shaking that was painful in its intensity. He turned his head in their direction, but he was looking not at herself but at Caroline behind her. In a kind of sick paralysis she waited as he made his way across the room towards them. Feverishly she searched his face for some discrepancy that didn't tally with his dream-image, but there was none. She knew his face as well as her own, and she had never seen him before.

Someone had put a glass in her hand and she drank quickly. Caroline was saying gaily, "Laura, this is the man I was telling you about, who used to live at Four Winds. Lewis Castleton, my sister-in-law, Laura Hardy."

His eyes, heavy-lidded and slate-grey, passed over her face without interest, but he said "How do you do?" pleasantly enough and held out his hand. She could no more have taken it than put her hand into a crocodile's mouth. She made some confused murmur about the glass she was holding, which he smilingly acknowledged before turning his attention back to Caroline.

At least, Laura thought a little hysterically, he did not appear to have had the same dream himself! But as she remembered the feel of his mouth and hands, so vivid in the dream, the dislike which had come with awakening intensified into actual nausea, scorching and stinging at the base of her throat.

Fortunately it was at that moment that Edward took her arm and introduced her to one or two people before settling her comfortably on a sofa next to an elderly lady who was their host's mother. Mechanically Laura made appropriate replies to her remarks, while her eyes returned with sick fascination to Lewis Castleton.

He was tall and broad-shouldered, with a tendency to stoop, and though he was dressed conventionally in a dark suit, it seemed to Laura's heightened senses that he was happiest in casual clothes and seldom wore a tie. Perhaps, she thought bleakly, that was just something else she instinctively knew about him. The dark hair was rather long, as she remembered, but it gave the impression more that he had not bothered to have it cut than that he cared for the present fashion. He bent his head to catch what Caroline was saying, and as Laura's eyes slid from him to her sister-in-law, their acute awareness of each other struck her forcibly. Caroline had never looked more beautiful, with her heavy gold hair swept up on top of her head, and there was a breathless, excited gaiety about her that sounded warning bells in Laura's head.

Anxiously she looked round for Edward, wondering how she could inveigle him to Caroline's side before the attraction that was flaring between her and Lewis Castleton should reach flashpoint. But he had disappeared in the crowd and her searching eyes couldn't locate him.

"Are you all right?" enquired a brusque voice on her left, and she turned quickly to see a tall, thin young man staring down at her almost belligerently.

"Oh, I—yes—yes, thank you."

"I noticed you when you came into the room. I thought you were going to pass out."

Laura moistened her lips and thankfully seized on her past history. "As a matter of fact, I'm just recovering from a rather unpleasant car crash. This is the first time I've been out since."

"I see." The piercing grey eyes didn't leave her face, and she had an uncomfortable suspicion that her half-truth

21

was only half-believed.

"May I join you?" he asked abruptly, and sat down before she had a chance to reply. "You're Edward Hardy's sister, aren't you? My name's Paul Denver."

"How do you do?" Laura said a little faintly.

"You're quite sure you're all right? Would you like me to get you a glass of water?"

"No, really, thank you. It's just—rather hot and noisy, isn't it?"

"It certainly is. Personally, I loathe these ritualistic occasions."

"Then why did you come?" she asked unthinkingly, and then, flushing, "I'm sorry—I didn't mean—"

But he gave a bark of laughter. "Don't apologize, it's a good question. I came because Mr. Howard has been good enough to print some articles I wrote on higher education."

"Not another journalist!" Laura protested, smiling.

"No, actually I'm a schoolmaster."

She turned at that and looked at the thin, bony face with its high forehead and intent grey eyes. "I should imagine you're a very good one."

His eyes held hers. "Thank you. I believe you're right!"

She smiled involuntarily. This forthright young man was a tonic after the denials and false modesties she was used to. "And where do you teach, Mr. Denver?"

"Ledbrook Boys' Grammar, for my sins."

"As bad as that?"

"Not really, no. They're an average bunch. Some respond, some don't. Others you know quite well could be brilliant if they'd put their minds to their work. They don't, of course, and it almost breaks your heart. Such waste!" There was a vehemence in his voice which told

22

her that this was a pet subject of his.

"And what subjects do you teach?"

"English and history. I might add that one of your father's novels is a set book for the third year this term!"

"Really? How interesting! Which one?"

"*The Sentinel.* It comes under the category 'Modern novel by well-known author.' Am I right in thinking you once wrote a book yourself?"

"Yes, but I doubt if that will ever be a set book!"

"Laura—" Edward was standing in front of them. "I'm sorry to interrupt, but I want you to meet Clive Sandilands. Clive—my sister."

Laura rose to her feet, Paul Denver beside her, as a rather short, pleasant-faced man came forward and took her hand.

"Miss Hardy. Edward tells me you're contemplating another book. I must say I'm delighted!"

"Thank you. Mr. Denver was just asking about my first, but I'm sure he'll be much more interested in yours. He teaches history. Paul Denver—Mr. Sandilands."

Paul's pale face was flushed with excitement. "It's a great honour to meet you, sir. I've admired your work for years. I was just telling Miss Hardy that one of her father's books is on the curriculum this year. I need hardly add that your historical analyses have been considered works of reference for as long as I can remember."

Clive Sandilands laughed. "Thank you. I'm grateful for the compliment, even if it does make me feel as old as the history I write about!"

Edward, who, to Laura's relief, had at last moved off in search of Caroline, now rejoined their circle with her, but Lewis Castleton came with them and more introductions were performed. Castleton was standing next to Laura, and as he bent forward to shake Clive Sandilands' hand, his sleeve brushed against her arm. She felt herself sway dizzily and with a surge of gratitude was conscious of Paul Denver's hand steadying her.

"Now, Clive," Edward instructed, "let's have your findings! Is your study of violence confined to the United States?"

Beside her, Laura was penetratingly aware of Lewis Castleton's sudden stillness.

"In this instance, yes," Sandilands was replying. "And it's also confined to the sixties—*The Violent Decade*, I'm calling it. Of course, the outstanding instances were the ghetto riots and the assassinations of public figures—the Kennedy brothers, Medgar Evans, Martin Luther King, Malcolm X. But I have a theory that they were only the tip of the iceberg, the outward sign of countless acts of violence some of which were never even recognized for what they were."

"Lewis," Caroline broke in eagerly, "didn't you say you were in the States at the time of Robert Kennedy's death?"

"Yes, I was, as it happens." To Laura's acutely attuned ears, his voice sounded strained, a little off key.

"Really?" Sandilands exclaimed. "That's fantastic! You weren't by any chance actually on the spot, I suppose?"

"Very nearly. I was over there to cover the primaries. I spent the whole of that evening with the rest of the press in room 516, just across the corridor from Kennedy's."

Clive Sandilands' eyes were shining with excitement. "You mean you were actually at the Ambassador? I can't believe my luck! Just meeting you by chance like this! Were you there when the shots were fired?"

"No." Lewis Castleton moved uncomfortably, but it was impossible to resist the other man's eagerness. He

24

went on rather reluctantly, "Kennedy came out of his room about midnight to go down to the Embassy Ballroom and claim the victory. The crowd had been chanting for him for hours. We all surged after him, but there was such a crush at the elevator—" he smiled slightly—"lift—that several of us gave up and went back to our room to watch it in comfort on TV."

"Go on, man!"

"It's all rather hazy, I'm afraid. I'd been drinking heavily, celebrating with the Kennedy crowd, and although I didn't know it, I was also on the verge of a breakdown."

"But you must remember something more?"

"Well, there was the speech, of course, and the crowd laughing and cheering. He started to make the usual tributes to his supporters, and at that point someone, his campaign secretary, I think, came in and said Kennedy would be leaving for The Factory straight after his press conference, so we all went down. And by the time we got there, it had happened."

"Incredible!" Sandilands said wonderingly. "Simply incredible! What was the first you knew about it?"

"Well, as I said, everything was blurred by this time. I remember the bedlam in the ballroom—screaming and sobbing and girls in campaign ribbons kneeling and praying. Then I regret to say I passed out completely. I didn't know anything else until I came to in hospital days later."

"What a scoop!" Edward said. "My God, what a thing to have experienced!"

Lewis Castleton emptied the glass in his hand. Laura saw that a muscle was jumping at the corner of his eye. "Yes. I never got the chance to write it up, of course, but plenty of other people did."

"It must have been a personal shock for you," Caroline

remarked, "having been so close to him."

"It was, of course, but the possibility of assassination was always there. Only the previous day a firecracker had exploded as they drove through Chinatown in San Francisco. His wife was terrified but Kennedy was perfectly calm." He glanced across at Sandilands and added sardonically, "Your *Violent Decade* in action."

"Yes, indeed." Sandilands seemed a little subdued by this first-hand account of the tragedy, and Laura warmed to him still further.

"Is it principally the political murders you're concentrating on, Mr. Sandilands?" Paul enquired.

"Not principally, no, but they naturally all tie in, the re-emergence of the Ku Klux Klan and the other side of the coin, the growth of the Black Power movement. But as I said, apart from those altogether there were literally hundreds of other instances reported daily in the press, without even taking into account those which interested me equally—reports of accidents, and so on, which were quite probably undetected murder. To give you a brief example, I found when I looked up the files for that first week in June when Robert Kennedy was shot that the headlines immediately prior to that had been full of the death of General Balfour's wife."

Laura jerked involuntarily as though an electric current had run swiftly through her body. "Balfour?" The name seemed to sound an echo in her mind.

"Yes, you probably read about it at the time. Clark Balfour was winning all the acclaim in Vietnam. Then he was seriously wounded and was actually being flown home when his wife was killed. Now, on the face of it that was a perfectly ordinary car crash, but there were one or two circumstances about it that interest me—so much, in fact,

26

that I intend to follow them up if possible when I get back to the States. For instance—Jumping Jupiter!" He broke off suddenly, a look of comic dismay on his face. "Whatever time is it?"

Edward glanced at his watch. "One-thirty, why?"

"I promised my assistant faithfully that I'd be on the one-forty-five to Charing Cross. Will you excuse me? I must find Tom and Patty. Look, I haven't really contributed much to Laura's research. Edward, how about bringing her and your wife to dinner with me one evening? I'm staying at the Westmorland Hotel in Cromwell Road. It'll have to be this coming week because we're flying back to the States on Saturday. How would Tuesday suit you?"

"Fine, as far as I know. Thanks."

"That's great. Sorry to rush off like this. I'll see you at the Westmorland, then, about seven-thirty on Tuesday? Delighted to have met you all!"

Laura discovered she had been holding her breath, and let it out in a long sigh. Edward glanced at her face.

"I think it's time we went, too."

Caroline said quickly, "While on the subject of dinner invitations, Edward, I did mention to Lewis that he must come one evening and see what we've made of his old home. When are you free, Lewis?"

Castleton was staring after Clive Sandilands and gave no sign of having heard her.

"Lewis?"

"I'm—sorry. Did you say something?"

"I was wondering when you're free to come and have dinner with us."

"That's very kind of you." He felt vaguely in his pocket for his diary. "I'll be most interested to see the house again," he went on after a moment, and again Laura was aware of the strain in him and the effort it took to drag his attention away from his own concerns to make polite conversation. "I'm sure you've done wonders with it. Is there still that collection of twisted old trees at the bottom of the garden?"

Of its own volition, Laura's hand felt for and fastened tightly onto Paul Denver's. She was aware of Caroline's startled eyes on her face.

"That's odd," Caroline said after a moment, and there was a note of uncertainty in her voice.

Lewis Castleton was flicking through his diary and looked up. "What is? Hoping those freak trees are still there? I used to spend most of my time climbing them when I was a boy."

Caroline said slowly, "There are no twisted trees in the garden now, and there weren't when we bought the house. But Laura saw them!" Her voice rang in accusation.

There was a brief pause while the three men looked at her in surprise. Then Castleton said reasonably, "I don't see how she could have seen them if they weren't there."

"Nor do I, but she did. Didn't you, Laura?"

Laura could only nod, unable to meet their curious eyes.

"The day she arrived," Caroline went on, "she looked out of the bedroom window and made some remark about twisted trees. I asked what trees and she said she was sure she'd seen some. For pity's sake, Laura, don't go clairvoyant on us!" Her laugh was brittle.

Paul Denver said briskly, "No doubt it can all be explained by association. It's quite a well-known theory, you know. Something reminds you of something else, and your brain assumes it's the same even though it isn't. For instance, at some time probably Miss Hardy—Laura—

28

looked out of a window and *did* see some trees like she described. So when she looks out of another window, perhaps years later, for an instant in her mind's eye she sees them again."

"Do you read the teacups too?" Caroline asked, with an edge to her voice.

"I believe we were trying to fix a date for Lewis to come for dinner," Edward remarked peaceably. "When are you free, old man?"

"Well, I was just telling Caroline that I've decided to buy Gillet's cottage, at the far end of Brocklehurst."

"Really? I'm glad you've found something you like."

"It's in pretty poor condition and I want to paint it throughout before I move in. I'd like to get that finished this coming week if I can, but any time the following week I'd be delighted to come."

Caroline extracted her own diary from her bag. "How about Friday the eleventh?"

"That would be fine."

"Good. Now, Caroline, get the coats, will you? Laura's almost out on her feet."

Paul Denver said, "I must be going, too. Good-bye, Laura. No doubt I'll see you again." Presumably his secret support of her during the last few minutes had allowed him to dispense with "Miss Hardy," and she was glad.

"Good-bye, Paul. Thank you."

When she turned from him, she saw to her untold relief that Lewis Castleton had disappeared. Edward was watching her anxiously.

"Not overtired are you, love?"

"A little, perhaps, but I'll be all right."

"I hope it wasn't a mistake to persuade you to come."

"At least I met Mr. Sandilands, which was half the

point of the exercise."

"He's a pleasant chap, isn't he? Dedicated to his work, of course. He seldom talks about anything else."

"Has he never married?"

"No, but I rather gather that the girl he speaks of as his 'assistant' assists him in more ways than one!"

"Really, Edward!" Caroline admonished lightly, handing Laura her coat.

"True, my love, quite true. I'll be interested to meet her. I believe she's a graduate of the American universities—a very intelligent young lady."

They made their good-byes and Laura was glad to relax in the back of the car for the fifteen minutes that the journey back to Brocklehurst took. She leant her head against the cushions, letting the others' voices wash gently against her eardrums. She had a great deal to sift through, but that must wait till she was in the privacy of her room after lunch.

"I see you allowed Paul Denver to cotton onto you, Laura," Caroline remarked over her shoulder. "I should have warned you about him. Rather an uncouth young man, I'm afraid."

"I liked him," Laura said defiantly. She refrained from adding that with his close-cropped hair and neat pinstripe suit she considered him far more 'couth' than Lewis Castleton.

"Very left-wing, I believe," Caroline said, with an air of having brought the subject to a close.

Laura smiled to herself.

"Incredible story, that, about Kennedy," Edward remarked after a moment. "I'd no idea Lewis had been there. I wish he'd been working for the *Courier* then!"

"It wouldn't have done you much good, since he collapsed at the crucial moment."

"I suppose not. And what was all that nonsense about Laura having seen some trees?"

"Just that she said she did, the day she arrived. That was weird enough, but when it transpired that they actually had been there once—"

Laura said jerkily, "I'll try to concentrate my powers on forecasting the Derby winner in future."

"I'd just as soon you'd no powers to concentrate," Caroline murmured feelingly as they turned into the gateway of Four Winds.

Chapter 3

CLIVE SANDILANDS' assistant proved to be decorous as well as intelligent, a slim, leggy American girl who was several inches taller than the rather short Sandilands, with swinging fair hair and round grey eyes behind enormous horn-rimmed spectacles.

"Fenella's been my right hand for the last five years," Sandilands said fondly. "She has a brain like a rapier and a wonderful capacity for skimming through mountainous piles of references and creaming off exactly the information we want."

"We could do with her in our office!" said Edward with a laugh. "Do you do any of the actual writing, Miss Gray?"

"She does," cut in Sandilands, "but she refuses to take the credit for it."

"Oh, but I only write the background parts that link the main events," she protested. She had a rather low voice, with the kind of soft American accent which is a pleasure to listen to.

"I may say," put in Caroline ruefully, "that as the only nonliterary member of this group, I have an outsize inferiority complex!"

They were sitting in the small cocktail bar of the Westmorland Hotel and Laura, away from Brocklehurst and all its associations, was relaxed and happy. She liked Clive Sandilands and she had felt an immediate affinity with the attractive Fenella Gray, who, she now decided, was

32

not quite as young as she had first thought—probably in her early thirties, but still a good fifteen years younger than her employer. Laura's eyes went from her to the man next to her, with his pleasant, rather highly-coloured face, thinning brown hair and suggestion of middle-aged spread. Strange how nature triggered off attractions between two such dissimilar people as the bustling, middle-aged scholar and the quiet, studious American girl. Shared interests had obviously been the starting point, but Laura conceded that Edward's comment that there was more between them was probably not far short of the mark.

Following her train of thought, she glanced across at Caroline, remembering her taut gaiety in the company of Lewis Castleton. Was there really danger there for Edward? For the first time, Laura found herself wondering whether her brother's marriage was happy or whether, during the course of sixteen years, either of them had strayed. As this new thought occurred to her, she realized that ever since her arrival at Four Winds she had been aware of a tightly controlled impatience in Caroline, which she had subconsciously put down to her own nuisance-value. But it was possible that quite apart from the inconvenience of her own arrival, Caroline was at present going through a restless and dissatisfied phase. If so, it was surely unfortunate that it should be at this particular time that she had come into contact with the unattached and obviously attentive Mr. Castleton.

She came back to her surroundings with the realization that they were preparing to go through to the dining-room. The Westmorland was one of the older, less pretentious hotels. It had been owned by the same family for fifty years and had a reputation for good if unimaginative food and a personal interest in the comfort of each guest.

The dining-room was small and rather old-fashioned, but their table was attractively laid, the highly polished silver winking in the light from the candles which stood in the centre.

Their order taken, Sandilands leant forward and clasped his hands on the table. "Now, Laura—I may call you Laura?—I'm interested to know why such a delicate-looking young lady should have a consuming interest in the subject of violence!"

Laura flushed and joined in the general laughter.

"She thinks," Edward said teasingly, "that she may have suffered a personality change as a result of a recent car accident."

"You were in a crash?" Sandilands asked.

"Yes. My mother was killed." Laura's hands interlaced tightly on her lap.

"I'm so sorry. Was this only recently?"

"Just after Christmas."

"Weren't you using some car crash to expound your theory on undetected violence?" Caroline interrupted, turning to Sandilands. "Just before you remembered you had a train to catch the other day?"

"Oh, the Balfour business. Yes, I believe I was."

"And you thought it might not have been an ordinary accident. Why was that?"

"Well, according to one report, the driver of a car Mrs. Balfour had passed minutes before the crash swore there were *two* people in the car. The police explored this possibility pretty thoroughly, but only the one body was found and the car certainly hadn't stopped in those few minutes. So if there *had* been someone else, who presumably escaped injury, why didn't he or she come forward? The obvious explanation, to my way of thinking, is that it must have been someone who didn't want his presence known— perhaps a lover? And remember all this happened while the General was actually being flown home."

"Was that suggestion ever put forward?" Laura asked.

"It's not the kind of thing they could put into print, especially with the wounded hero desolate over his young wife's death."

"Was there anything else?"

"Yes, apparently there were one or two reports that the car was weaving about erratically for some moments before the crash—time, anyway, for a couple of motorists to phone the police and report it. So why didn't this mysterious companion take over the wheel? Or did he attempt to, thereby causing the crash? One thing I'm positive about— if it hadn't been for Robert Kennedy being shot a couple of days later, the Balfour business would have been gone into much more thoroughly by the press. The police, of course, kept working on it, but no more was ever reported except the inquest verdict of accidental death. And to digress for a moment, what a stroke of luck running into that chap at Tom's! Almost an eyewitness account of the assassination! I was sorry afterwards that I hadn't included him in my invitation for tonight, but then I could hardly have left out the earnest young schoolmaster and our intimate little gathering would have been considerably stretched. But let us return to our sheep."

"Does this violence bit interest you too, Miss Gray?" Edward asked with a smile.

"Fenella, please! Well, I guess so indirectly, but I'm more concerned with the corresponding sociological conditions between phases of violence in the past and those of the present day. If we can find some link between them, we might be onto something big."

35

"Edward has the somewhat naive idea," remarked Caroline rather caustically, "that it's all due to the fact that there hasn't been a war lately to absorb man's natural aggression."

Fenella smiled. "As an American, I should have to qualify that. There's hardly been any time since nineteen forty-five when American forces haven't been engaged somewhere in the world fighting in the interests of democracy."

"And the maintenance of law enforcement," intoned Edward nasally, "or was that only U.N.C.L.E.?"

Sandilands said, "But it's a novel, surely, that Laura will be working on, which will give her a lot more latitude than we have, keeping strictly to the facts. Have you any idea how you'll set about it?"

"Not really." She pushed away her plate. "I think perhaps I might write round a central character who has been in all the trouble spots over the last twenty years, a mercenary, or someone like that."

"If that's the way your mind is working," Edward commented, "you could hardly do better than to talk to Lewis Castleton. He's never been a mercenary as far as I know, but as a journalist he's been wherever, to coin a phrase, history has been made. You heard him yourself on Robert Kennedy, and I know for a fact he was in Vietnam, Kenya, the Middle East—he was even in Munich during the Olympic games massacre."

Caroline said brightly, "Perhaps you could have a word with him when he comes to dinner next week."

"Then," said Sandilands, "if I can't be of any more help, let's change the conversation to more pleasant topics! Has anyone any strings to get us seats for Drury Lane either tomorrow or Friday? I know we've left it very late, but a spot of light relief would be more than welcome. Failing that, any theatre that's not showing a murder play would be most acceptable!"

At ten o'clock Edward put down his coffee cup. "Would you think us rude if we left you now, Clive? It takes a good hour and forty minutes to get home, and that will be quite late enough for Laura. She still needs a lot of rest."

"Not at all. Of course you must go whenever you're ready. It's very good of you to have come all the way here to have dinner with me. I'll get your coats."

They moved out into the hall together.

"Where did you leave the car?" Sandilands enquired.

"Down some little back alley behind the hotel. It's not far away."

"I'll come along and see you off."

"No, don't bother. You haven't a coat down here."

"Nonsense. It's a mild spring evening and I could do with a little exercise after that meal. Fenella, order another pot of coffee, will you? I'll only be five minutes."

It was very dark down the alley alongside the hotel and they linked arms to steady each other on the uneven surface. Occasional lights from the windows high up in the wall shed sporadic pools of brilliance which only intensified the surrounding darkness. They turned left and then right and came upon the car in the narrow little street where they had left it.

"Keep me posted about the progress of the novel," Clive Sandilands instructed, "and the best of luck with it. I'll be in touch once we've settled down again."

They shook hands and the three of them climbed into the car. Its headlights sprouted tongues of light, illuminating the small figure of Sandilands waving them off. Then they had left him behind and were threading their way through the narrow streets and out again into the well-lit thoroughfare of Cromwell Road.

"What a charming man he is," Caroline observed. "I can quite see why Fenella finds him attractive."

They talked intermittently between themselves and in the back seat Laura closed her eyes and let herself drift towards sleep, her body swaying from side to side with the movements of the car.

There were no lights on in Brocklehurst when eventually they reached it, and the looming shapes of the houses, dark against the paler sky, had a foreboding about them which made Laura shudder, chilled as she was after her cramped half-sleep. However, the lantern-shaped light at the gateway of Four Winds welcomed them home and as Edward drew up outside the front door, the sudden ringing of the telephone, sinister in the sleeping house, reached their ears.

"Who the hell can be phoning at this time of night?" Edward demanded irritably, hurrying to put his key in the lock.

"Quickly!" Caroline urged. "It'll wake Peter!"

Edward strode ahead of them into the hall and Laura was closing the door behind herself and Caroline when the tone of his voice altered drastically.

"*What?* Oh, my God! How did you—?"

Caroline caught at his sleeve. "Whatever is it?"

He shrugged her off, glancing at his watch. "Look, I'll come straight back. I can be there by about one. . . . Are you sure? Who's with you now? Can they give you a sedative? . . . Well, if you're absolutely sure, because it would be no trouble. . . . Yes, all right then. I'll be there about nine o'clock. Try to get some sleep."

Slowly he replaced the receiver and stood staring down

at it, his face paper-white.

"For heaven's sake, Edward—" Caroline began jaggedly.

He turned clumsily to face them. "It's Clive. He's dead."

"*Dead?*" Caroline's voice rose an octave. "But he can't be! We've only just—" She broke off.

Laura felt her legs give way. She sank down onto the monk's bench, staring unblinkingly at her brother.

Edward was speaking jerkily. "He didn't come back from seeing us off. God, if only he'd stayed at the hotel! That last little act of courtesy cost him his life."

"But what *happened?*" Caroline demanded.

"He just didn't come back. Fenella had ordered more coffee as he'd asked, and after about ten minutes she went outside and looked up the side alley but couldn't see any sign of him. She became anxious and sent the doorman out to look."

Edward's trembling hand went to his forehead. "He found him lying sprawled in the alley. Of course, they thought he'd just collapsed, but—when they finally got him back to the hotel, they discovered he'd been stabbed, just once, through the heart."

"*Stabbed?*" repeated Caroline. "You mean—it was murder?"

Laura's fingers were pressing against her shaking lips. Not Clive Sandilands—not that polite, helpful little man—

"But why?" Caroline whispered.

Edward shook his head helplessly. "It looks like a mugging. His wallet was taken, and his gold watch."

There was a long silence while they all stared at each other, desperately trying to deny the truth of what they'd

39

just heard. At last Caroline moved. "It looks as though the seventies are to be *our* violent decade," she said, "but Clive won't be here to write about them."

The story of the murder made the later editions of the papers the next morning. Seeing it in black and white finally and irrevocably convinced Laura of the appalling truth. Soon after ten o'clock Edward phoned from London, but he had nothing further to report. The police were working on it, but it looked as though they hadn't much chance of finding the murderer. He had tried to insist on Fenella's coming to Four Winds, but she had held out against it. It was understandable; although they were her last link with Sandilands, she had only met them the previous evening. She was extremely calm, Edward reported, and seemed capable of handling everything necessary. In the circumstances all he could do was return to Ledbrook. He had been interviewed by the police and they knew where to reach him if they needed him.

At twelve o'clock the phone rang again, and Laura was surprised to learn it was for her.

"Laura? Paul Denver here. I've just heard the news on the radio. Is it true? About Mr. Sandilands?"

"Yes," she answered dully, "quite true."

"But weren't you to have met him last night for dinner?"

"We did. It happened after he had seen us off."

"God, it's unbelievable!"

"I know."

"Are you all right? You sound pretty shaken."

"Well, of course I'm shaken. If I hadn't—" She broke off and fought to steady her breathing.

"Now look, it's bad enough without you starting to

40

imagine things."

"I'm not imagining them, Paul; they're true."

There was a pause, then he said abruptly, "Are you free this afternoon?"

"I suppose so. I usually rest in the afternoons."

"I have a free one today. I'll come and collect you and we'll drive around a bit. Okay? It'll do you good to get out for a while." She didn't make any comment. "Laura? Will you come?"

"Yes, all right," she answered apathetically.

"I'll be round in a couple of hours."

She was waiting for him at the gate when he arrived in a rather battered-looking Ford, and they drove for several minutes in silence before, with a quick glance at her face, he said in his usual abrupt manner, "Do you want to talk about it?"

"I've nothing to say. It was all in the papers."

"There's nothing you can add?"

"No, except that if I hadn't said I was interested in violence he wouldn't have invited us to dinner and it would never have happened." The words came out in a rush.

"In which case," Paul said deliberately, "he would probably have fallen under a bus instead."

"Meaning his time had come? You really believe that?"

"I'm not sure what I believe, except that you can't consider yourself even remotely responsible for his death. But that doesn't alter the fact that it's a terrible business, a brilliant man like that at the height of his success."

"I know. Oh, I know."

They drove on a few more miles and then, completely changing the direction of her thoughts, he said almost conversationally, "Are you going to tell me why the sight of Lewis Castleton frightens the living daylights out of you?"

41

She caught her breath and shot him a startled look. "Did it show that much?"

"I'll say. Every time he came near you, you nearly flaked out. Now, while he's not my type, I've never considered him in quite the same light as Count Dracula!"

He glanced at her with raised eyebrows, inviting a smile, but she was staring down at her twisting hands. He waited, guessing she was trying to decide how much to confide in him.

At last she said quietly, "You said a minute ago you didn't know what you believed in. How about—precognition?"

"Ah-ha! The old 'I've been here before' syndrome. I think it's generally accepted nowadays that such a thing exists, more widely than most people realize. Go on."

She kept her eyes on her hands. "The day I came to Four Winds I dreamt about Lewis. Four days before I even knew of his existence."

When she didn't continue, he prompted, "And is that so very terrible?"

"It is to me." She shuddered.

"What exactly did you dream?"

"It was horrible."

"And that's all you want to say about it?"

She flushed. "Yes. I'm sorry."

"Could it be taken in any way to suggest you might be in danger?"

"No, I suppose not."

"You are quite sure about dreaming it?"

Her eyes flicked up. "Of course!"

"I only ask because one theory is that due to some mental quirk, a part of the brain might register something a split second before another part, with the result that when the second part sees it for the first time, it already looks familiar."

"Not in this instance." She shook her head decidedly. "I was thinking about it all week. I couldn't get it out of my head."

"Did you feel it was 'horrible' while you were actually experiencing it? Was it like a nightmare?"

Her flush deepened. After a long moment she said quietly, "No."

"And presumably you also dreamt about those trees?"

"Oh no, I actually *saw* them. Caroline confirmed it, didn't she?" She gave a shaky laugh. "No doubt by now you're convinced I'm quite mad!"

"On the contrary, it's all most intriguing. By some means or other you managed to 'see' trees which weren't there, only to learn later that they once had been. An interesting point arises: Did you in that flash see into the *past*, when the trees actually had been there, or into the future, to the moment in time when you yourself heard about their existence? Do you see what I'm getting at?"

"I think so. Does it matter which it was?"

"It could. Do you know anything about Dunne's theory of serial time?"

"Nothing whatever!"

"Well, it's very complicated, but the essence of it is that there is more than one time dimension."

Laura said apologetically, "If you're going to launch into physics, I'm afraid I'll be way out of my depth."

"You wouldn't be alone in that! It was the dream business that made me think of Dunne, though. He carried out all kinds of experiments with volunteers who guaranteed to write down, immediately they awoke, everything they could remember dreaming about. These records were conscientiously gone through every day for about a month, and an incredible thing emerged. The dreams were almost equally divided between those that referred to things that had happened in the past and those that referred to the future. In other words, although we don't realize it, we're as likely to dream of the future as of the past, because in another dimension of time it has already happened. Most of the Oriental philosophies embrace the concept of the Everlasting Now, in which past, present and future co-exist."

He glanced at her bewildered face and gave an embarrassed laugh. "Sorry, it's the schoolmaster coming out!"

She said slowly, "It's a fascinating thought, but why don't people *realize* they've been dreaming about the future?"

"Because—and this is the crux of the whole thing—ninety-nine per cent of dreams are completely forgotten within minutes of waking. That was why Dunne insisted they had to be written down immediately. Just occasionally something happens which reminds us of what we've already dreamt, and we say it's 'broken the dream.' You see, Dunne's point was that so-called precognition and clairvoyance are not the gifts of a selected few but are within the scope of anyone who cares to exercise them."

"Well, I for one don't!" Laura declared roundly, "but perhaps I haven't any option."

"Obviously some people are more sensitive to atmosphere than others—it would be easier for them. You said just now that you dreamt about Lewis Castleton the day you arrived at Four Winds. Wasn't that about the time you saw the nonexistent trees?"

She looked at him quickly. "Yes, it was. The two things probably happened within an hour of each other."

44

"It could almost be a case of telepathy, then. You'd somehow 'tuned in' to Castleton's mind. He could easily have been thinking about the house and garden—after all, we know Caroline had already mentioned the possibility of his going to dinner."

"And—the other?"

"Perhaps another episode in his past. Did you actually figure in the dream yourself?"

She hesitated for a moment. "Now that's very interesting. I'd forgotten that part. It *felt* like me, but he called me something else. After all, if it was something out of his past, it couldn't have been I, could it?"

"What did he call you?"

"I'm trying to remember. A rather unusual name— Noel! That was it."

"I suppose you've never known anyone by that name?"

"No. The interesting question is, has Lewis Castleton? Paul, do you think there *could* be a connection between my dreaming about him and the fact that he once lived at Four Winds?"

"It's possible, though I don't quite see how, unless houses have 'memory banks' like computers! Is there anything about the house itself that disturbs you?"

A tremor ran through her and he turned the car off the road and drew to a halt. "What is it, Laura?"

"More of my infernal psychic powers, I suppose," she answered with a touch of bitterness, but he noted that she had gone pale.

"Hadn't you better tell me?"

"There's not much to tell. It's just that all the time I'm in the house I'm strongly conscious of a feeling of de- spair—a cold, desperate unhappiness. Nobody else seems to notice it."

45

He smiled crookedly. "You don't go in for half-measures, do you? All we need now is 'things that go bump in the night'!" He laid a hand over hers. "Have you told anyone else?"

She shook her head. "It's not a thing you want to advertise."

"I think perhaps you should. This—unhappy feeling. If it's really strong, it might be a case for exorcism."

She recoiled violently. "No!"

"Laura, it's not healthy for you to be surrounded by all this when you don't want to be. Let me have a word with Edward—"

"No!" she said again. "Don't you see, they wouldn't believe it, and who could blame them? They've noticed nothing themselves. They'd just think I needed a course of psychiatric treatment or something, and I've had enough of hospitals to last me a long time. And that reminds me. Dr. Banstead gave me a note to take to Edward's doctor and I haven't yet."

"Then will you tell him what you've told me?"

"Certainly not! He'd have me committed!"

"Don't talk like that!" Paul said sharply.

She turned to face him. "Paul, you've got to promise me not to repeat anything that I've told you."

"But I—"

"Promise!" she repeated.

"All right," he said reluctantly, "if you feel you can cope."

"I shall have to, shan't I?"

"You've never had any of these kinds of experiences before?"

"Not before I came here, no. Perhaps my weakness after the accident has made me susceptible, I don't know."

46

"Well, will you promise *me* that if it—gets out of hand at any time you'll let me know?"

"What could you do?"

"Talk some sense into you, perhaps, and make you see the doctor."

She said quietly, "Is there a prescription to banish ghosts? I've just thought—your Everlasting Now would help to explain them, wouldn't it? They've just strayed over their own time barrier."

"It would probably explain a lot of things." He looked at her anxiously. "Had I better take you home now? You're looking rather tired."

"Yes, I'm probably missing my rest. I've enjoyed the drive, though. Thank you for asking me."

"I hope you'll come again," he said formally.

They turned in a wide arc and started back in the direction of Brocklehurst, both of them busy with their own thoughts. A few minutes later Paul turned in between the wrought-iron gates and Laura subconsciously braced herself. The brief respite was over and Four Winds was waiting to claim her again.

Chapter 4

LAURA'S talk with Paul Denver had hardly reassured her, and returning to a household still shattered by Clive Sandilands' murder in no way helped to restore the balance. During the remainder of that week, the police were in touch with them several times. The post-mortem had revealed nothing new; Clive Sandilands had been in reasonably good health for a man of his age, though his heart was slightly enlarged. Death, due to a knife blade penetrating the cardial cavity, had been instantaneous. There was a bleak comfort in that.

Laura duly presented herself at Edward's doctor's surgery and handed over the letter from Dr. Banstead, which he read carefully. Dr. MacIntyre was a tall, quietly spoken Scot with a receding hairline and compassionate brown eyes.

"And how are you feeling just now, Miss Hardy? Are the headaches any less frequent?"

She hesitated. "Yes, they are. In fact, I don't think I've had one since I came to Brocklehurst ten days ago."

"Well, that's very good news. You still seem a trifle tense, though. Is anything else worrying you?"

"Not really, Doctor."

"I heard of your brother's friend's death, of course. That must have been an added shock for you."

"Yes."

"You're sleeping well?"

"Quite well." She smiled a little. "I'm afraid, Doctor,

that like the rest of my family I have rather more than my share of imagination. It can be a curse as well as a blessing!"

He smiled back. "I'd rather not prescribe sedatives or tranquilizers unless you really need them, but if you do, please don't hesitate to call me. In the meantime, I'll drop in to have a look at you occasionally when I'm passing, to satisfy myself you're making satisfactory progress."

She nodded and stood up. "Thank you." For an instant more she hesitated, tempted after all to tell him something of her fears, but he had already pressed the bell for the next patient and her chance had gone.

The funeral took place that Saturday. Edward insisted it was unnecessary for either Laura or Caroline to go, and they were secretly relieved by his decision. He returned from it impressed afresh with Fenella Gray's calm courage. She had delayed her return to the States by one week in order to attend the inquest the following Monday, and was hoping to leave on the Saturday after that. In the meantime, she had again politely refused his invitation to come to Four Winds.

With their lives so bound up in Clive Sandilands' tragedy, Laura had completely forgotten that Lewis Castleton was invited to dinner that Friday. Obviously, though, Caroline had not. On Thursday morning Laura looked into the kitchen to find her busily engaged in making pastry. Since Mrs. Baines did most of the cooking, this was unusual enough to cause comment.

"I'm preparing the first course for tomorrow," Caroline replied.

"Tomorrow?"

She turned, pushing her hair back with her forearm since her hands were covered with flour. "Lewis is coming. Had you forgotten?"

"Oh, of course! Yes, I had, actually." She paused. "It doesn't seem quite right, somehow, to be having a dinner party when—"

"You mean we should observe a period of court mourning?" Caroline asked sharply. "Clive would be the last person to want that. Anyway, it's hardly a party—only Lewis."

Laura watched her as she turned back to the pastry board. Lewis Castleton was returning to Four Winds, she told herself deliberately, and waited for the expected tide of apprehension and distaste. Surprisingly, it did not come. In fact—and she found it hard to accept—she was aware of a feeling of pleased expectancy. No doubt it was merely the anticipation of an evening which would not be spent gloomily going over the funeral or the inquest.

The following evening as she was changing for dinner, she was suddenly aware of someone watching her and turned sharply, surprised to see that the intruder was a small boy, staring at her with large blue-grey eyes.

"Hello!" she said, startled. "Are you one of Peter's friends?"

The child didn't answer. He seemed puzzled by her presence. After a moment, swinging on the door handle, he said confidentially, "Grandma's dead. I've just been in to have a look at her."

Laura stared at him, uneasiness beginning to prickle her scalp. "You must be mistaken," she said at last. "Your grandmother doesn't live here."

"Of course she doesn't *live* here—she's dead!" His matter-of-factness and complete absence of grief struck Laura as callous and unchildlike. She said a little more sharply, "What's your name?"

He stared at her for a moment frowningly and then, either bored by the conversation or resentful of her tone, slipped out of the room, and after a moment, rather disconcerted, she went on brushing her hair.

Lewis Castleton had arrived by the time she went down. He and Caroline were standing close together as she opened the sitting-room door and they moved swiftly apart.

"Oh, there you are, Laura," Caroline said a little breathlessly. "Edward's just gone for some ice. Did you—?" She broke off as Edward himself came in with the ice bowl.

"Do sit down, Lewis. Now, gin and tonic, wasn't it?"

"Thank you. I was just saying how attractive you've made this room. I remember it as rather dark and forbidding, with a Victorian horsehair sofa, of all things!"

"We'll show you round later. How's the decorating going?"

"I'm beginning to see the light at last!" He leant back in the easy chair, crossing his legs. Once again he was dressed formally and Laura felt that the conventional collar and tie irked him. "Didn't know the place had so many windows, though! I'll have to forage around to find some curtains. I've no wish to live in a goldfish bowl!"

"I doubt if you'd get many people going past, though," Edward remarked. "It's a bit of a dead-end down there, isn't it?"

Caroline said eagerly, "As a matter of fact I've a lot of material left over from the curtains I made for this house. I hadn't realized the fabrics were sixty inches wide. If you let me know your window measurements, I'll run several pairs up for you."

"Oh, look, I really couldn't—"

"But why not? Provided the colours fit in with your

decor—"

Lewis Castleton laughed briefly. "Decor? Rather a grand name for emulsion paint!"

"Then there's no problem."

"But I can't take up your time—"

"I'm a lady of leisure, Lewis," Caroline retorted gaily, "and my time's my own! I'm delighted to think the material won't be wasted after all."

Laura dragged her eyes away from the two of them to accept the glass Edward handed her. Was he aware of this growing attraction between them? she wondered. If so, he certainly gave no sign of it. She wished there were some way of warning him without saying too much.

"You have a son of fifteen?" Lewis was repeating. "I don't believe it!"

Caroline flushed prettily. "True, I assure you. And a daughter of thirteen."

"Really, Edward, I didn't know you'd been guilty of cradle-snatching!"

"I was married just before my twentieth birthday," Caroline admitted. "Even the baby's nine now. It makes me feel ancient!" Her low laugh intimated that it made her feel no such thing.

"Better not let him hear you refer to him as 'the baby'!" Edward commented. "By the way, where is he?"

"At Cubs—it's Friday, remember. If you go and collect him at eight, we can eat as soon as you get back."

Laura stirred. "Peter's not home? Then why was that other little boy here?"

"What other little boy?"

"The one who came to my room while I was dressing. I assumed he'd come back with Peter."

Caroline said impatiently, "I don't know what you're

52

talking about. There's been no child here this evening."

"If Peter's to be picked up at eight, I'd better go now." Edward drained his glass and put it on the cabinet. "Shan't be long."

He went out of the room and Lewis and Caroline resumed their conversation—about, Laura discovered when she bothered to listen, furniture, curtains, the advantages and otherwise of living in a village. Obviously her reference to the boy upstairs had been dismissed out of hand, but her mind continued to circle round the incident. Possibly he was someone connected with Mrs. Baines who had called at the house without Caroline being aware of it. But his remark about his grandmother— She was glad enough to have the riddle to puzzle over, since it meant she could shut herself away from the low voices across the room.

Edward reappeared in due course and Peter made a dutiful appearance before being sent to the kitchen for milk and biscuits. To Laura's surprise, the anticipation which she had found herself looking forward to this evening evaporated, leaving her flat and depressed. Silently she followed the others into the dining-room, marvelling a little sourly at the care and attention that Caroline had lavished on the room. The massed flowers, the gleaming table and shining glass and silver all combined to give an impression of relaxed well-being and enjoyment and the meal itself was superb. None of which dissipated her growing irritation with Caroline, whose flirtation with her guest was becoming, Laura felt, increasingly blatant. She was even glad when the conversation turned momentarily to Clive Sandilands, since it interrupted their exclusiveness.

"They didn't get far at the inquest," Edward remarked. " 'Murder by a person or persons unknown.' I could have told them that myself."

"I was shocked to read about it," Lewis Castleton said smoothly. "I only met him that once, but he seemed a charming and brilliant man. It's ironic, really, that he should die like that. Almost as though his preoccupation with violence had somehow rebounded on him."

"What a macabre idea!" Caroline said with a shiver.

"There's one thing," Edward said; "his work won't be wasted. Fenella says she has all the notes and intends to go ahead and publish the book posthumously."

"Fenella?"

"His assistant, Fenella Gray. She's collaborated on all his books for the last five years."

"I see. I heard him mention his assistant, but I hadn't realized anyone else was so closely involved with his work. Will she be staying on in this country?"

"No, she's flying back to the States tomorrow. She is American, anyway."

Peter put his head round the door. "I'm going up now, Mum."

"All right, darling, sleep well."

Laura said suddenly, "Peter, did any of your friends come here this evening? To borrow a schoolbook or anything?"

He shook his head. "Don't think so. 'Night." The door closed behind him.

"For heaven's sake, Laura, what is this? I told you—"

"I know what you told me," Laura interrupted, "but the fact remains that a little boy *did* come to my room this evening. Actually, it was rather unpleasant. He said his grandmother had died and he'd just been in to see her."

"Well, really!" Caroline began, but Lewis's voice cut across hers.

"That's odd!" There was a jerky note in his voice. "My grandmother died in this house thirty-odd years ago. To the day, in fact, if I remember correctly."

There was a short, uncomfortable silence, then Edward laughed briefly.

"I imagine many people's grandmothers have, over the years."

"Yes, but the curious thing is that I sneaked in to see her, just as Laura's—apparition reported."

"Dear God!" said Caroline faintly.

Laura, tensed and waiting, was concentrating all her attention on Lewis Castleton. The flatness and depression had suddenly gone and she was aware of being on the brink of something strange and exciting. He was staring back at her, registering her, she felt, for the first time, and when he spoke to her, his voice held that note of exclusive attention that he had previously kept for Caroline.

"What did he look like, Laura, your little boy?"

Like you, she thought, oh, God, like you! "He was small and dark," she faltered, "with blue-grey eyes and"—memory stirred—"a green hand-knitted sweater."

"Yes," said Lewis softly, "incredibly enough, I remember that sweater."

"Great heavens, Lewis!" Caroline's voice cracked. "I hope you're not trying to imply that you're engaged in haunting this house!"

He dragged his eyes momentarily away from Laura. "Oh, nonsense. But it was my home once, remember. It's rather nice to think there's still a part of me here. Still, I can hardly haunt you, can I, when I'm very much alive."

"But your childhood isn't," Laura said unexpectedly, and their eyes turned with a fearful fascination back to her. She felt obliged to elaborate and went on a little uncertainly, "There's no reason why spirits should always be as they were at the moment of death, surely? I was discussing various theories of time with Paul the other day. If, as some people believe, time is running continuously on different levels, then we'd all have several 'ghosts' to our credit, wouldn't we, of the past and of the future and therefore both older and younger than we happen to be at this present moment?"

"How chilling!" Edward said softly. He glanced across at his wife's white, frightened face and reached for his glass. "Well, all I can say, Lewis, is that I'd be grateful if you'd refrain from allowing your alter ego to alarm my sister!"

"Your sister doesn't seem to be unduly alarmed," Lewis said, his eyes still thoughtfully on Laura. "Could it have been the little boy who showed you the trees?"

"No," she answered seriously. "I had never seen him before."

Caroline's chair scraped back. "For God's sake stop them, Edward! Are they mad, or am I?" She was almost in tears.

"Yes, that's enough, you two." Edward lifted the decanter. "More wine, Lewis?"

"No, really, thank you. That was an excellent meal, Caroline."

"Coffee's in the sitting-room," she said stiffly. She rose from the table and, without waiting for them, went quickly from the room. After a moment's hesitation Laura followed her and as she reached the hall, Caroline's fingers dug painfully into her arm.

"I hope you're satisfied, now that you've ruined my evening!"

"But, Caroline, I didn't—really. I'm sure no one—"

56

"Just like a nasty little child who hasn't been getting enough attention!"

"Very well, I'll leave you to have your coffee in peace. Please say good night to Lewis for me."

Astonished at her own composure, Laura ran lightly up the stairs, rounding the bend just as the men came out into the hall below. As she pushed open her bedroom door, the strangely buoyant confidence that had been with her for the last few minutes exploded into a brief, illuminating burst of sheer happiness. It lasted only a second, but she slept more soundly that night than at any time since the crash.

Before he left for work the next morning, Edward phoned Fenella to wish her bon voyage and to ask her to let them know if they could be of any help. The weekend stretched rather flatly ahead and Laura, uncomfortable in the face of Caroline's continuing coolness, was relieved when Paul Denver phoned.

"Do you feel up to the cinema and supper afterwards?"

"I'd love it, Paul. Thanks."

In the moment of meeting, his keen glance raked her face. "How are things?"

She pulled the car door shut. "All right."

"Did you go to the doctor?"

"Yes. He didn't say much."

"And what did *you* say?"

She smiled. "Not much either!"

"As I feared! And what else have you been doing since I last saw you?"

"Lewis Castleton came for dinner last night."

"Oh, dear, and I wasn't there to hold your hand! How did it go?"

She gave a little shudder. "It was strange, Paul. I can't

57

describe it. At the time, I was actually glad he was there!"

"Well, that's a turn-about for the books!"

"But I don't understand it. I still dislike him intensely. Just thinking about him now makes my flesh crawl. And yet last night—" She shrugged helplessly.

"What actually happened?"

"I rather think I must have had another one of my 'time lapses,' and as usual Lewis was tied up with it." She went on to tell him as factually as she could of the little boy's appearance and Castleton's interpretation of it. "Is it feasible, Paul?" she finished. "Could he have been a ghost out of time? The idea gave Caroline hysterics, and I must admit in the clear light of day it sounds ludicrous, but last night, with Lewis just across the table, it seemed the obvious solution."

Paul said slowly, "God knows, but it's becoming increasingly clear that there's some connection between you, though I'm damned if I know what it is. I don't like it, Laura. All these—manifestations, for want of a better word, seem to have the effect of drawing you closer together. The dream you won't tell me about made you aware of him in the first place, and the business about the trees made him aware of you. Now this—"

"Yes," she said in a low voice. "I see what you mean. I hadn't thought of it like that. It's almost as though, against our will, something's pulling us together."

"What about that unhappy aura you were conscious of in the house? Are you still aware of it?"

"We've all been so depressed about Mr. Sandilands lately that a bit more misery wouldn't have been very noticeable." She paused. "Actually, though—"

"Yes?"

"It's ridiculous, really, but it did strike me last night

58

that she was actually happy for a change."

" 'She'?"

" 'It,' then." She shivered. "Can we talk about something else?"

"All right. I just wish, though, that there was some way of ensuring that you needn't see Castleton again."

Caroline, having ascertained the measurements of Lewis's windows when he phoned to thank her for Friday, spent most of the weekend making curtains, and the fifth pair was duly finished on Tuesday morning. That evening she phoned him to arrange when to take them round. The obvious step of his calling himself to collect them was never even mentioned, Laura noted wryly.

"He has to be away for the day tomorrow," she told Laura when she returned with heightened colour from the phone, "so it'll have to be Thursday. He has a friend coming that evening to spend a couple of days with him, so I said I'd go round after lunch and help him to hang them. I don't suppose he has much idea how to go about it."

On Thursday, however, Caroline's careful plans were thrown completely out of gear by a telephone call from Peter's school at lunchtime. Peter had been accidentally hit on the head by a cricket ball and they were taking him straight to the casualty department of the local hospital. Could Mrs. Hardy meet them there?

Caroline stood irresolutely in the hall, obviously torn between anxiety for her son and bitter disappointment at not being able to go to Lewis as arranged.

"Couldn't you take the curtains tomorrow?" Laura asked, in a last attempt to deny the calm certainty that was growing inside her.

"That'll be too late. His friend will be there tonight."

59

Laura drew a deep breath. "Then I'll have to take them, won't I?"

"You?" Caroline hesitated and glanced at her watch. "All right—there's nothing else I can do. If you're ready now, I can drop you off at the bottom of Gillet's Lane. You can't walk all that way with the heavy curtains. Explain what's happened, won't you?"

Lewis Castleton was, of course, surprised and, Laura felt, annoyed to see her instead of Caroline, but he had to accept her explanation and also her offer to help him hang the curtains.

"Caroline has pinned a note on each pile, to say which measurements are which," she said as she unwrapped the brown paper parcels on the only clear surface she could see in the cluttered room. The ceiling of the cottage was so low that Lewis stooped even more, and the windows, small and diamond-paned, hardly looked big enough to warrant curtains at all. Against the walls were packing cases full of strange shapes wrapped in newspaper, and large piles of books and papers lay heaped on the floor.

"As you see, I'm not exactly settled," Lewis said shortly, following her glance. He had still not forgiven her for not being Caroline. "I've ordered a large desk which will take a lot of that stuff, but of course it hasn't arrived yet."

Laura shook out the folds of the first pile of curtains. "We put some hooks in—we didn't think you'd have any."

"No, I haven't."

"We'll have to hold the curtain up to the window to decide how much to ruche it."

"To what?"

"Ruche—pull it together, like this. These two pairs are

the same measurement. Which pattern do you want in here?"

"God knows. Whatever you've got there will do."

They worked side by side for the next hour, mostly in silence, measuring, ruching, inserting the hooks and finally hanging the curtains. There were only four rooms in the original cottage, two up and two down, but a bathroom extension had at some stage been added behind the kitchen. There was no hall; a wooden staircase went straight up from a corner of the living-room. Very little furniture was in evidence—a bed and chest of drawers in Lewis's own room and a camp bed put up, no doubt for his expected visitor, in the other upstairs room. A couple of chairs stood rather bleakly against a wall.

"Home sweet home," Lewis said sarcastically, and again she realized guiltily that he had intercepted her rather disparaging glance.

"At least it all looks bright and fresh with the new paint," she offered placatingly.

"I warned Harry he'd have to take me as he found me. We were out in Biafra together for a few months and I haven't seen him since. Anyway conditions here are slightly better!"

Biafra. Laura stood dreamily with a pair of curtains over her arm, imagining the whining bullets, the humidity of the thick forests, the sudden explosion of bombs— violence, violence which he'd seen at first hand. A memory stirred of Edward saying, "You should speak to Lewis—"

"Come on or we'll never get through," Lewis broke in on her thoughts. "Is this the last pair?"

"Yes. Sorry." Working beside him, watching his strong

61

hands with the black hair on the backs of them, she felt strangely at peace, relaxed as she had never felt at Four Winds—except, she realized with a surprised tremor, the night he had been there. Odd how, at Four Winds last Friday and again now, she should all at once feel resigned—more than resigned, acquiescent, to whatever might follow. Mistily she remembered the revulsion she had spoken of to Paul, but it had no meaning here.

Together they hung the last pair of curtains and Lewis stepped back, wiping his hands down the sides of his old corduroy trousers. In them and the rather ancient open-necked shirt which he wore, he looked much more as she remembered him. "Remembered"? She pulled herself up sharply. She had only seen him twice before and each time he had been wearing a dark suit.

"Well, I for one am ready for a cup of tea. How about you?"

Without waiting for her reply, he went clattering down the wooden stairs ahead of her, whistling tunelessly. Laura followed him slowly and stood in the centre of the living-room arching her aching back and looking round for a spare chair. This was the most energetic afternoon she had spent for a long time.

Through the tiny diamond window-panes a shaft of sunlight struck like a pointing finger, alighting on one of the piles of books along the wall. Idly she went over and picked up the topmost book. It seemed to be a scrapbook of some kind, a conglomeration of old photographs and press cuttings with Lewis's name at the head of the columns.

"Come and get it!"

She carried the book with her into the kitchen and laid it down on the breakfast counter, hoisting herself up onto one of the stools. Lewis was rinsing the milk bottle under the tap and standing it on the draining board. He hadn't turned as she came in. Resentfully, she thought, "He wouldn't be so offhand if I were Caroline!" and surprised herself by the latent jealousy in the thought. She, who didn't even like him!

He leant over her shoulder to plonk a mug of steaming tea in front of her, and an electric tingle ran through her. "What have you got there?"

"Please let me look—that mention of Biafra has aroused my interest. You must have had a fascinating life."

"That's one word for it." He hitched himself up beside her, drinking from his own mug, which had no handle. Everything in the room was suddenly exceptionally clear, as though bathed in a hard white light, and her other senses quickened to the same pitch. She could smell the faint, aromatic odour of the tea, the tobacco which clung to his clothes, and hear the drip-drip of the tap he had not turned off properly. It was as though the whole room held its breath, waited to see what would happen.

Her hand was trembling as she slowly turned the pages of the scrapbook—yellowing newsprint, war pictures. She didn't know what she expected to see. Then suddenly she had found it, and her breath came out in a long sigh. Alone in the centre of an otherwise empty page was a snapshot of a girl, a girl with fair hair drawn smoothly back, a broad forehead and wide eyes set slightly slanted in her face. Her mouth was curved in a smile of singular sweetness, as though it were someone very special at whom she smiled. The eyes in the photograph stared straight up into Laura's own and she gazed back unmoving. It was as though she were looking into a mirror at her own face, though the girl bore no physical resemblance to her at all. Beside her Lewis Castleton sat as still as she, his eyes like hers locked on the page in front of them.

Suddenly Laura moved, closing the book and pressing her hand down on top of it. "Lewis—this book I want to write—" Her breath was coming so rapidly that she had difficulty in speaking. "Will you help me with it? Please?"

His eyes hadn't changed focus, were still staring down where the photograph had been and her hand now lay. With an effort he said, "What on earth are you talking about?"

"I must—oh, please!" The words were falling unintelligibly over themselves and, sensing his rising impatience, she struggled to regain control. "Will you let me write about you? Your life story? A sort of official biography?" She laughed breathlessly. "I've been wanting to write about violence, and you've seen so much of it. Edward said that wherever anything's been happening for the last twenty years, you've been there."

"I must have a word with Edward."

"Lewis, please say I can! Please let me talk to you and use your war diaries and scrapbooks—it all looks so alive in here!" Her hand moved caressingly over the dun-coloured cover.

He said slowly, "It was enough to live through it once."

She caught frantically at his arm. "Don't you see I've just got to do it? I think this must have been what everything was building up towards. Paul said there was something—"

He frowned and shook her hand away. "Paul? I can't imagine what—"

"No, I know. It doesn't matter. All that matters is that you let me write your life. Oh, Lewis, you will, won't you?"

He stared down at her wild, pleading face, disconcerted by her anxiety. "Look, I haven't seen any more than dozens of other men—"

"Please, Lewis!" Tears were coursing down her face now but she seemed unaware of them. Embarrassed, he turned away.

"Oh, for pity's sake, write the damned thing if it means so much to you!"

"I can?" Her voice rose tremblingly. "Oh, that's wonderful! How can I thank you?"

"You don't need to thank me. I suppose I should be flattered that one of the famous Hardys wants to write about me. And now it's high time I took you home. I hate to think what interpretation Edward would place on the state you're in! Get your coat, there's a good girl, and we'll go."

He almost bundled her out of the cottage and into the car which stood in the lane outside. Her face was like wax and she was trembling violently. From time to time as they bumped along the rough surface of the lane he glanced at her anxiously. At the gateway of Four Winds he drew up and waited for her to climb out. She said through shaking lips, "Can I see you tomorrow?"

"Not tomorrow, Harry'll be here. Leave it till the weekend—perhaps Saturday."

She nodded vaguely, turned away and walked up to the house. For a moment he sat staring frowningly after her. Then with a shrug he started up the car.

PART 2

Caroline

Chapter 5

"YOU MEAN to tell me you let Laura go and hang those infernal curtains?" On Edward's face incredulity battled with growing anger. "Really, Caroline, I'd have given you credit for more sense! No wonder the child's exhausted!"

Caroline's temper snapped. After all the anxiety, disappointment and frustration of the day behind her, Edward's righteous indignation was more than she could stomach.

"She's not a child, to start with, though the way you all dance attendance on her she might well be, and a backward one at that! I told you I took her in the car and Lewis brought her back. She was only out for a couple of hours."

"And you can see the state she returned in!" Edward retorted angrily. "An hour or more bending and stretching and holding up the weight of those curtains would wear anyone out, let alone someone who—"

"Oh, for God's sake, Edward, let it drop! Heaven knows, I wanted to go myself—" It was rich, she thought on a spurt of furious, inward laughter, that she should have to explain to Edward that she had wanted to go to Lewis. Lord, how she had wanted! She remembered, with a belated twinge of conscience, that her thoughts on the way to the hospital had been more of disappointment at missing Lewis than worry about her injured son.

"Apart from anything else," Edward went on, "I always have the impression she doesn't care for Lewis anyway.

I've caught her watching him like a rabbit does a snake."

"Charming!" She spun the wheel of her lighter furiously. "A nice way to speak of our friend, I must say! The way you're carrying on I might have been guilty of pushing Trilby into Svengali's clutches! She *offered* to go, I keep telling you!"

Edward looked at her for a moment and she saw the fight drain out of him. He turned away wearily. "Do you have to dramatize everything?"

"I?" She gave a hard choke of laughter. "My dear Edward, where Laura's concerned, you're the one who dramatizes endlessly—probing, sifting, worrying. God, don't you know how sick I am of having that girl in the house, and she's only been here a fortnight!"

Edward said flatly, "You've always been jealous of Laura, heaven knows why."

"Jealous?" She paused in the act of denial. "Perhaps I have, in a distorted kind of way, but in all conscience the reason's plain enough. She always comes first with you, before me or any of the children."

"Now you're just talking nonsense."

"I'm not, you know, and it's time you faced up to it." She threw back her head and exhaled a cloud of smoke. Her eyes when they came down to his were hard and bright. "Do you know what my first memory of Laura is? No doubt you've forgotten the occasion, but it was hardly designed to set us off on the right foot, looking back on it."

He met her brilliant, challenging gaze warily. "I can't say I remember, no."

"It was the day we became engaged. You took me back to meet your parents and I was a bundle of nerves. I hadn't slept at all the night before. After the initial ordeal

70

of the introductions, you took me over to where Laura was sitting on a stool in the corner. I can see her now, she could only have been about six or seven. And you took my hand and said, 'This is Caroline, Laura. What do you think? Shall I marry her?' " She broke off, fighting to control her breathing.

Edward moved uneasily. "Well, it was only a joke, for God's sake."

"A joke! In front of your whole family? Richard and Toby were there too. And I had to stand and wait, feeling like I don't know what, while that little chit looked me over with those great saucer eyes of hers and eventually said offhandedly, 'If you want to.' "

Edward smiled in spite of himself. "Did she really?"

"Yes, she did. And only then did your parents come forward to kiss me, as though they'd actually been waiting for her approval! Given the chance, I'd have put her across my knee there and then, and I may tell you I've often had the same desire since!"

Edward felt in his pocket for his pipe. "I admit it was a bit tactless, but it never occurred to me you'd resent it, let alone allow it to colour your whole relationship with her. Heavens, I wasn't much more than a kid myself at the time. It's perfectly ludicrous to have built it up to these proportions."

"But it wasn't an isolated incident. Time and again we all had to defer to her. Richard and Toby are just as bad. They dote on her as much as you do." She moved over to the window and stood staring out, arms crossed. "It was your parents who started it, of course. They idolized her because at last, after three boys, they had a little girl. I must say, it's lucky you were all so well-adjusted or you might have resented her furiously. As it was, you merely

71

followed your parents' lead. To give her her due," she added, turning back into the room, "she's turned out reasonably well, considering that by now she must have come to expect her own way in everything!"

Edward was staring at her. "My God, if I'd realized you felt as strongly as this about it, I'd never have suggested she come to live with us. Why on earth didn't you tell me?"

She said levelly, "Because if you had to choose between us, I'd no doubt you would have chosen her."

"Caroline!" He started towards her, but she instinctively stepped back.

"Anyway, if I'd refused to let her come, you'd never have forgiven me, would you? Remember how you put it? 'As head of the family, what else can I do?' And you also said it probably wouldn't be for long because she was sure to get married soon. Well, her illness hasn't done anything for her looks, and personally I can't visualize a queue of admirers lining up in the foreseeable future."

"Young Denver seems quite smitten."

"Oh, him!" Caroline stubbed out her cigarette contemptuously. "A jumped-up little nobody who talks like Al Reade!"

"Oh, Caro, come on! He might have a hint of a northern accent, but that's all, and what's wrong with that, anyway? He's a steady, sensible fellow, from all accounts."

"Well, if you consider him good enough for your precious sister, who am I to argue? Lord knows if he'll be able to support a wife, though."

"Aren't you rather rushing things? They've only met a couple of times."

"Yes, but he knows on which side his bread's buttered, I don't doubt! These Socialists always do!"

72

Edward lost his patience suddenly. "Now that's enough, Caroline! I've seldom heard such nonsense as you've been talking for the last ten minutes. I'm sorry you resent Laura, but once she's got her strength back, she'll find a job and only be in in the evenings, and then perhaps you'll be able to cope better."

"I consider I'm coping, as you call it, admirably well already."

"But tying yourself in knots while you do. Try to relax. Perhaps she can go to Toby and Janet for a while to give you a break. I'll have a word with Toby about it. In the meantime, I'm going up to sit with Peter for a few minutes. Were they quite happy about him at the hospital?"

Typical! Caroline thought resentfully. Having criticized her for exhausting his sister, he can now afford to give a little thought to his son! But she was tired of rowing with Edward. It was like beating her head against a brick wall anyway. She merely replied, "He has to stay at home quietly tomorrow, but he should be able to go back to school on Monday."

Edward nodded and left the room and Caroline resumed her restless pacing. If only she could have gone to Gillet's this afternoon! It would have been the first time she'd been alone with Lewis. Heaven knew when there'd be another opportunity. Had he been disappointed when Laura had arrived instead?

She frowned and lit another cigarette. Actually, she had to admit that Edward had a point about the effect her apparently strenuous afternoon had had on Laura. When she herself had arrived back from the hospital with the white-faced Peter in tow, Mrs. Baines had told her Laura had returned sometime previously and gone straight to her room. Anxious for news of Lewis's reception of the curtains, she had gone straight up, but Laura had been un-communicative to the point of idiocy. There was a glazed look in her eyes and she had answered monosyllabically all Caroline's impatient questions.

Against her will, Caroline suddenly remembered the occasions when she had felt less than comfortable in Laura's presence—the uncanny incident of the "little boy" with whom Lewis had so ridiculously identified, the trees which she had seen in the garden. She gave a superstitious shiver. Three hundred years ago Laura would probably have been burned at the stake, she thought grimly as she went to see about the evening meal.

Laura had elected to stay in bed for the rest of the evening, and conversation during dinner was stilted, both Edward and Caroline wary of each other and still going over in their minds the unpleasant scene in the sitting-room. As soon as they had finished, she slipped upstairs to see if Peter had settled and was relieved to find him asleep and the colour creeping back into his cheeks. They had assured her at the hospital that it was the shock which had upset him rather than the actual impact of the ball which, it transpired, had fortunately only struck him a glancing blow.

She hesitated on the landing outside Laura's door and, hearing no sound, tapped lightly and eased the door open. Laura, too, was sound asleep, a curious little smile on her lips. Caroline stood for a moment looking at her, trying to come to terms with her resentment. The thin, pale face and the tumbled hair spread over the pillow made her seem much younger than she was, hardly older in fact than in that first, bitter memory she had at last confided to Edward.

When she returned to the sitting-room, it was to find

74

Edward settled for the evening in front of the television. She paused, her restlessness still tormenting her. The room felt close, and outside the last of the evening sunshine was gilding the new green leaves.

"I think I'll just take the car out for a run," she announced abruptly.

Edward turned in surprise. "Why on earth?"

"I don't know. I feel all tensed up, and driving always relaxes me. I won't be long."

"Okay, suit yourself." He turned back to the set. In the hall Caroline caught up the coat she had dropped on the monk's bench earlier when she came back with Peter, and, feeling in the pocket for the car keys, let herself out of the front door. She stood for a moment breathing deeply. It was much milder than it had been earlier in the day, and she remembered with a sense of surprise that it was already May.

She wound the car window down, wishing momentarily that she had a sports car and could set off roofless down the country lanes. Gradually, as she drove, she felt herself begin to relax, enjoying the breeze which lifted her hair. The sun which had lured her out had set now and the air was thickening slightly with the approach of dusk. She had no idea where she was going and she slowed down a little, contentedly cruising along and letting those in a hurry pass her by. She rounded the bend in the road by the Three Bells and suddenly all her tensions returned in full force and she jammed her foot on the brake, causing angry tooting from the motorist behind who had narrowly missed going into the back of her car. She hardly heard it, her eyes on the blue sedan parked at the end of the row. That, beyond shadow of doubt, was Lewis's car. Lewis was inside the pub now. She had only to go through that door to be with him. The blood was thundering in her ears. Dare she go in? She had the curtains as an excuse—she was anxious to know if they'd been exactly right.

Perhaps it would be better to drive on. For all her sophistication, Caroline Hardy had never been into a pub by herself in her life. But she wouldn't be alone for long. He might even suggest she come round to see the curtains for herself tomorrow. Trembling a little, she turned the car's nose in beside the blue sedan and before her courage failed her, walked quickly across the concrete and pushed her way through the door.

A wave of heat and smoke hit her as a crescendo of sound clogged her ears. For a moment she stood blinking, getting her bearings, and a group of farmers at the near end of the bar turned round and nudged each other, whistling appreciatively. She was on the point of retreat when, across the curve of the bar, she caught sight of the back of Lewis's head. She would have recognized it anywhere, the way the thick dark hair fringed the collar of his shirt and the broad, slightly bowed shoulders. Her heart seemed to be in her throat as she inched her way through the crowds until, rounding the bar, she came face to face with him. He was talking to a short, fair-haired man, but the force of her gaze raised his eyes to hers and for a long moment they stared at each other. Then he straightened slowly and she went the last few paces towards him.

"Well, Caroline! This is a pleasant surprise!"

She said awkwardly, "I was passing and saw your car, so I thought I'd just pop in and see if the curtains were all right."

"I'm glad you did. Harry, this is the lady who so kindly—what's the expression?—'ran up' my curtains for me. Such an ambiguous phrase, I always feel! Caroline

Hardy, Harry Tait."

Harry—of course! The friend who was staying with him, whose advent had occasioned the need for the curtains in the first place. A wave of disappointment washed over her as she turned to Harry, who was regarding her with open curiosity and approval.

"How do you do?" she said a little stiffly.

"What'll you drink, Caroline? Gin and tonic?"

"Please."

Lewis turned to the bar and Caroline, finding Harry Tait's eyes still on her, groped for something to say to him. "Will you be in this country long, Mr.—?"

"Harry'll do, my dear. Harry'll do. No, just till Saturday, actually. Then I'm off to Brussels for some specialist reporting on the Common Market. I was just telling Lewis here how surprised we all were that he'd come back to this country and even gone as far as buying a house. He was always the most footloose of us all, but I can see that this district has its attractions!" He winked at her and she looked hastily away and took the glass Lewis was holding out to her.

"Did Laura manage the curtains all right?" she asked hurriedly. "I'm sorry I couldn't come myself."

He leant casually on the bar beside her and she was breathlessly aware of his nearness as, had she but known it, Laura had been before her.

"Yes, she made a very stout effort for such a frail little thing. She looks as though a puff of wind would blow her away, doesn't she?" He tilted his glass and stared down at the swirling liquid. "Did she tell you she wants to write my biography?"

"What?" Her face spun towards him. "Laura does?"

He looked up, meeting her startled eyes with a faint

smile. "Didn't she mention it?"

"No, but I've hardly seen her. When I got back from the hospital—"

"Of course—forgive me. I was forgetting. How is Peter?"

"All right, thank God. It wasn't as bad as it sounded on the phone. But when I got home Laura had gone up to rest and I haven't had much chance to talk to her since. When did all this come up?"

"This afternoon. She was looking through some of the scrapbooks that were piled on the floor waiting to be sorted out."

"You didn't agree, surely?"

"I rather think I did, eventually. Not that it matters much one way or the other to me, and she seemed very set on it."

Caroline was silent, wondering how this development would affect her own relationship with Lewis. Would they have more chance to meet if Laura were writing about him, or less?

Lewis added smilingly, "I suppose I have to admit to being rather flattered."

Caroline said, "Of course, it's the violence she's interested in"—and broke off, flushing.

Lewis laughed. "Well, that's put me in my place!"

"I'm sorry, I only meant— Look, I must go. I told Edward I wouldn't be long. It was—nice to meet you, Mr. Tait."

Lewis straightened and put his glass on the bar counter. "I'll see you to the car."

"There's no need—" But he gave her a little push and she started to make her way back through the crowded room, her temples pounding. She shouldn't have come—

she had only looked foolish—why hadn't she just kept on driving?

As they came out into the cool near-darkness, she said shakily, "I'm sorry. I spoiled your evening with your friend."

"You don't really believe that." His voice was low and she felt herself start to tremble again.

"Lewis, I—" But he had taken her arm and drawn her into the patch of shadows round the corner of the building.

"You mustn't take any notice of Harry," he said softly. His hands came up to her shoulders, kneading them under the light coat. "He couldn't matter less." And then, on a kind of groan, "Oh, God, Caroline!" and he pulled her roughly against him, his mouth harsh and demanding. She gave a choked little cry as her arms flew round his neck, straining herself against him while wave after wave of scalding weakness washed over her, draining every ounce of strength and will power. At last his mouth moved onto her face, her hair, her throat, and with a supreme effort she managed to push him away.

"No, Lewis! Not here!"

"Then where? When?" His hand cupped her chin and he kissed her again, holding her head rigid until he had finished.

"Not now!" She could hardly speak, but a car turning off the road had briefly illuminated them with its headlamps and recalled her to their position. "Lewis, Harry's waiting!"

"Damn Harry to perdition!" He pulled her close a little less urgently, brushing his lips over her face. "He's leaving first thing on Saturday. Can you find any excuse to come to the cottage?"

79

"The curtains?" she whispered against his mouth.

"The wonderful, marvellous, quite fantastic curtains! And I haven't thanked you for them yet, either."

Just round the corner from them the bar door swung open on a burst of sound and several people came out, laughing and talking as they made their way to their cars. Reluctantly, almost painfully, Caroline moved away from him. His hand reached out and held hers tightly.

"When will you come?"

"I don't know. Perhaps after shopping, on Saturday morning?"

"I won't move from the house all day!"

Their eyes strained toward each other through the dusk.

"Good night, Lewis."

"Good night, Caroline." He lifted his hand and touched her hair, then they walked together round the corner and he pushed his way back into the bar. The wave of noise and light spilled out toward her as though trying to draw her back, before the door swung shut behind him. For a few moments she leant, weak and trembling, against the cold stone wall. Then she pushed herself away and walked unsteadily to the car. Once inside, she gripped the wheel with both hands and rested her forehead between them.

"Oh, God!" she whispered. "Oh, God!" It was out in the open now. No more demure, averted gazes, no more wondering whether he felt as she did. He did, and they had acknowledged their impatience to each other. The sick trembling buffeted her whole body. The passion his kisses had aroused in her was beyond her experience, aeons away from the placid, pleasurable contentment which had been her response to sixteen years of Edward's lovemaking. This was something savage and essentially selfish, something that left her ashamed but crying out for more.

In a dream she forced herself to put the key in the ignition and, hardly knowing what she was doing, drive
slowly back home.

Edward was propped up in bed reading when she went
upstairs. He raised an eyebrow as she came into the
room, but she avoided meeting his eye and he made no
comment. Swiftly, trying to conceal her shaking fingers,
she undressed and took a shower, gradually turning the
tap until the icy needles stung her body with the impact of
a hailstorm. She was still saying, "Oh, God!" under her
breath, over and over like an endless litany.

As she slid between the sheets beside Edward, he
reached up and switched off the light. They lay side by
side in silence while their light-dazzled eyes gradually ad-
justed to the outlines of the darkened room. After a few
minutes, Edward stretched out a hand.

"Sorry, love," he said gruffly, "I didn't mean to fly off
the handle."

She had stiffened at his touch, her mind turbulently
boiling at the memory of Lewis's hands. She forced herself
to say briefly, "I'm sorry too." Sorry for the way I betrayed you tonight, for the way I intend to go on betray-
ing you, sorry, sorry. The word meant nothing.

"Fine. 'Night." And Edward, innocently convinced that
all was well again, turned unsuspectingly on his side and
went to sleep. But Caroline lay stiff and unmoving, her
eyes wide open while she made one final, half-hearted attempt to purge Lewis Castleton from her thoughts, knowing that the battle was lost before it had properly begun.

Chapter 6

A s i t happened, Caroline did not manage to go to the cottage that Saturday. She slept late the morning after her meeting with Lewis, having fallen into a deep sleep just as dawn was paling the sky, and she did not even hear Edward leave the house for work. She awoke finally at nine o'clock to the sun streaming onto the bed and the telephone on the table beside her jangling stridently.

She pushed back her heavy hair and reached for it, with the half-formed hope that it might be Lewis, but the brisk masculine voice said succinctly, "Caroline? Richard. How's Laura?"

"Laura?" She was still struggling free of the last strands of sleep. "Much the same as when you last phoned. Up and down."

"Um. Okay if Gilly and I descend on you for the weekend?"

"Oh—I—yes, of course." As long as she could lose them tomorrow morning. Tomorrow— Richard was talking and she forced herself to attend.

". . . so we can be with you around six."

She frowned, having lost the thread. "This evening?"

"Most assuredly this evening. And by the way, don't worry about making up two beds—we shan't use them. 'Bye, Caroline, see you later." The phone clicked in her ear. Slowly she replaced the receiver and lay back again. Damn Richard! Why should he be so free when everyone else was bogged down with some responsibility or other? Bogged down? She? In view of what she was planning?

She stared resentfully at the ceiling. She was conventional enough to have the prospect of her affair with Lewis marred by the voice of conscience and fleetingly envied Richard his apparent lack of it.

She swung her feet to the floor and stretched luxuriously, mentally going over the planned weekend meals in view of the additions to the household. She would go into Ledbrook this morning and do most of the weekend shopping, leaving only a few things over for tomorrow, to serve as an excuse to get out of the house to meet Lewis.

Laura was still at the breakfast table when she reached the dining-room. Caroline sat down and poured herself a cup of black coffee. "And how are you today?"

"All right, thanks."

"No ill effects after your tiring afternoon?"

"No. How's Peter?"

"He seems all right. He's curled up on his bed with a comic. By the way, that was Richard on the phone. He and his—girl are coming for the weekend."

Laura's face lit up. "Oh, lovely! What time will they get here?"

"About six, he said. I must get Mrs. Baines to air the bed." She sipped her coffee. "What's all this about your writing Lewis's biography?"

Laura's eyes shot to her face. "How did you hear about that?"

Damn, damn, damn! "I had to go out last night and happened to bump into him with his friend."

"Harry Tait. Yes, they were together in Biafra a few years ago. In fact, Lewis saved his life."

"Really? Did he tell you that?"

She looked vaguely puzzled. "I suppose he must have done."

"It wasn't mentioned last night, but I dare say it's hardly the thing that comes up in ordinary conversation. Tell me, what made you pick on Lewis?"

Laura smiled slightly at her choice of words. "I think it was actually Edward who suggested him when I first said I was thinking of basing the book on a central character who'd come up against a lot of violence. Then, when I looked through Lewis's scrapbook yesterday, it all seemed to come so fantastically alive—almost as though I'd been there myself and could recognize different scenes. I knew then that it was something I had to do. The worst part was trying to convince Lewis!"

"I can imagine," Caroline said drily. "And when do you propose to start work?"

"Probably tomorrow, I think."

"Tomorrow?" The word jolted out of her in alarmed surprise.

"Oh, of course, I can't now, with Richard and Gilly coming."

"Did Lewis suggest tomorrow?" Caroline enquired carefully.

"Yes, he said Harry would have gone by then. I'll have to let him know."

Caroline went on drinking her coffee, her mind churning. He must have forgotten all about the arrangement when he suggested she should also go round. How cozy it would have been if both she and Laura had turned up on his doorstep! Fortunately Laura would not now be going, but she didn't intend to let her visitors stand in her own way.

They arrived, breezy and unapologetic, at eight o'clock, thereby ensuring that the dinner had dried up in the oven. Caroline bit back what she considered her fully justified annoyance and welcomed them civilly but Richard, putting her gently to one side, went straight to his sister. He took both her hands and studied her face anxiously.

"Laurie! All right, honey? You don't look all that good."

"I'm all right. It's lovely to see you again. And Gilly." She smiled across at the slight, red-haired girl. Really, Caroline thought in exasperation, where does he find them? Gillian was wearing a curious full-length dress in browns and oranges and a selection of beads and bangles. Her hair gave the impression of having been absent-mindedly chewed by a succession of hairdressers, since it was layered all the way down the back of her head, finishing in a wispy straggle below her shoulders. The fact that the whole incongruous mixture added up to an effective and attractive whole Caroline could hardly deny, but she resented the casualness of the girl, which made her own tailored linen seem ultra-smart and sophisticated, as though she and not Gillian were striving to make an impression.

Richard had his arm across Laura's shoulders and was leading her to the sofa. "Come and sit down and tell me what you've been doing. Are you sure you're resting enough? Did you go to the doctor with Banstead's note?"

Caroline watched him resignedly. He was, without doubt, the best-looking of the three brothers, with wide candid eyes beneath straight brows and a firm, sensitive mouth. His toffee-coloured hair was midway between the dark brown of Edward and the light honey colour of Toby and Laura, but his attractiveness was in his manner as much as his appearance. It was his gift to make every woman, even his sister, feel she was the only one in the world that he cared about. Every woman except Caroline herself. Whether this was out of some idea of loyalty to Edward, she had never fathomed, but she always felt a little piqued that he had never, by so much as a flicker of an eye, betrayed any appreciation of her own charms.

He had been a boy of seventeen when she first met the family, two years younger than herself, but the fresh-faced charm that made women love him had been apparent even then. Caroline would willingly have entered into the half-bantering, half-flirtatious relationship which could be enjoyed innocently enough between brother and sister-in-law, but to her secret chagrin Richard had shown no inclination other than to accept her as Edward's fiancée and then wife. He had treated her from the first with an off-hand politeness which baffled and needled her.

"I'm afraid we really must go and eat now," she said. "The meal has been ready since half-past seven. I hope it will be all right."

"Oh, we're used to eating cinders!" Richard remarked casually from the sofa. "Gilly doesn't profess to be a cook, do you, love? Everything's either burnt or half-raw. I've always said I must have a cast-iron stomach!"

"Well, for those of us who haven't," said Caroline tightly, "let's go in to dinner."

Mrs. Baines had had a word or two to say to Caroline about the result of the delay on her carefully prepared meal, and Caroline feared that her displeasure, always inescapable once incurred, might create an uncomfortable atmosphere when she brought in the dinner. She had reckoned without her brother-in-law.

"Hello, Bainsy! You're not going to be crossed with us for being late, are you?"

"It's not my place to be cross, Mr. Richard," she replied severely, but her eyes were beginning to twinkle.

"That's my girl!" and the preposterous Richard leant

forward and kissed her soundly on her smooth round cheek.

"Really, Mr. Richard! Away with you!"

But Caroline had seen the genuine affection in the glance which followed him as he laughingly joined them at the table.

Laura, whose usually pale cheeks were flushed with pleasure, was only picking at her food and Caroline noted both the guests watching her anxiously. She felt unaccountably criticized, as though she personally should have seen to it that Laura's appetite had improved before this.

"We'll have coffee in the sitting-room; it's more comfortable," she remarked at the end of the meal.

"If you don't mind," Laura murmured, "I think I'll go straight upstairs. I'm feeling a little tired."

"May I come up in a few minutes and sit with you for a while?" Gillian asked. "I won't stay long, but we've not had a chance for a chat yet."

Laura smiled at her. "Do—I'd love that."

Edward led the way across the hall. "I thought it might be an idea to drive out to the Inchcape for lunch tomorrow and spend the afternoon in that area. It's a long time since we've had a day out."

"I won't be free in the morning," Caroline said, her voice a fraction higher than usual. Why the hell did he—?

"Oh? Why? What's on?"

"Well, the shopping, for one thing."

"I thought you said you'd been into Ledbrook today?"

"I did, but there are still a few things—"

"A few things are no problem. We can pick them up before we go or on the way back. Don't be a spoil-sport, Caro. I thought you'd be glad to have one less meal to worry about."

"Well, personally, I think it sounds a marvellous idea," Richard said lazily, settling himself in an easy chair. "I'm all for short, concentrated doses of country air, provided they're not too frequent!"

Fuming inwardly, Caroline took the coffee tray from Mrs. Baines. Something always seemed to come up to prevent her going to the cottage, almost as though the family knew about her obsession with Lewis and was determined to keep her from him. Like a continuation of her fancy, Richard leant back in his chair, crossed one leg high over the other, and said without preamble,

"Now tell me—who the devil is Lewis Castleton?"

It was so apposite that Caroline's hand shook involuntarily as she poured the coffee and it spilt on the silver tray. She bent forward hastily to mop it up with her handkerchief, screening her burning cheeks.

Edward was saying easily, "A chap I know. Why?"

"Apparently Laura's set her heart on writing his biography."

"No! Caro, did you know about this?"

She wasn't to be trapped a second time. "She did mention it, over breakfast," she murmured truthfully.

"What's he like?" Richard pursued.

"Oh, pleasant enough, I think. Restless kind of a chap— never seems able to relax. I don't know much about him, except that he used to live in this house."

"Really? What an extraordinary coincidence! You don't think Laura's going to fall for him or anything, do you?"

Caroline tasted the spurt of warm blood on her tongue.

"My God, I hope not! Whatever gave you that idea?"

"Just something about the way she speaks of him—it's not easy to pinpoint."

"For one thing, he's far too old for her. I must say this has all come as a complete surprise. I had the distinct impression that she didn't like him. In fact, I almost fancied she was afraid of him at one time."

"*Afraid?*"

"It sounds idiotic, doesn't it, and obviously I was wrong or she wouldn't be contemplating doing his life story."

Richard was frowning as he stirred his coffee. "She told me she hadn't liked him at first, but then she added that since he agreed to let her write the book, she's felt happier than she's ever been before. You know, Edward, there's something about this whole business that I don't much care for. I can't put my finger on it, but she's—different, somehow."

"If you ask me," Caroline put in jerkily, "I think she's psychic or something. That night Lewis came for dinner—"

"Oh, for God's sake, Caroline!" Edward exclaimed impatiently. "Don't bring up all that rigmarole again!"

Richard leant forward. "What rigmarole? I'd like to hear." He fixed his clear, impersonal gaze on Caroline and even then, confused and upset as she was, a part of her registered and resented his indifference. In as few words as possible she told him, almost sulkily, about Laura's conviction that she'd seen a child upstairs and the conversation which followed at dinner. Then, with a defiant glance at Edward, she mentioned the episode about the trees in the garden.

Richard sat motionless for some time after she'd finished, staring down into his empty coffee cup. At last he said, "Doesn't it strike you that there may be some odd kind of link between them?"

"Link?" Caroline repeated sharply.

Edward said, "Now for heaven's sake, Richard, don't start working out one of your complicated plots round all this. Young Denver had a perfectly reasonable theory to explain the tree bit, though I can't for the moment remember what it was, and as for the rest—well, she's tired and run-down and she overreacts, that's all."

"And what is it she overreacts to?"

"Hell, I don't know! Atmosphere, attitudes—"

"Let's get it straight. According to Laura, the boy had actually done what this Lewis bloke had himself done on the same night thirty years before. J. B. Priestley, here we come!"

"It does sound a bid odd, put like that, but—"

"And the fact that he lived in this house, I think, is very relevant."

"How do you mean?"

"Well, he actually remembered the trees. Therefore that part could have been unconscious telepathy. In the other instance, it is more as though—and I admit this sounds way out—as though *she* reminded *him* about it."

"That's ridiculous!" Edward said, but there was a note of hesitancy in his voice. "And I don't see how it could have been telepathy, either, since at that stage they hadn't even met."

"Yes, I'd forgotten that point. Look, Edward, one thing's obvious. We must get her away from this house. For some reason it seems to be harmful to her."

"My God!" Edward said abruptly.

"Now what?"

"I'd forgotten all about it—I only put it down to weakness at the time, but the day she came, I had the hell of a job to get her inside the house at all."

The other two stared at him. Caroline said slowly, "I

90

remember now, you did say something about it."

"Tell me exactly what happened," Richard demanded.

"Well, she was all right in the car, right up to the time we got out. I took her arm and opened the front door, and suddenly without any warning she went rigid. Then she started to gasp and struggle and fight to shake me off, for all the world as though I were trying to inflict some ghastly injury on her. I could hardly control her. After a minute she simply went slack and I carried her in."

"And that was all?"

"Isn't it enough?"

"It certainly is. That settles it. We'll take her back with us. She certainly mustn't stay here."

Edward said slowly, "I doubt if she'd go. If you'd come a week ago, she'd probably have leapt at the idea, but now that she's got her head full of this book—"

"At least I can try. I must admit I'm consumed with curiosity about this man. Is there any chance of meeting him while I'm down? I'd like to watch their behavior towards each other, for one thing. Quite apart from anything else, she's in a vulnerable condition emotionally and I feel we should vet anyone she comes into regular contact with."

Caroline said evenly, "Then you'd better vet that obnoxious young schoolmaster, too."

"And who's he?"

Edward started to explain and Caroline stood up abruptly. "If Richard's really set on meeting them, we'd better have them in for drinks on Sunday, and a few other people too or it will seem rather odd."

"Right, fix it, will you, Caro?"

She went into the hall, closing the door behind her and leaning against it for a moment. Of all the ridiculous nonsense—but at least it would give her a chance to phone

Lewis and warn him that she wouldn't be able to see him the next day. She hesitated by the phone in the hall and then ran lightly up the stairs to the bedroom and closed the door. Her fingers were trembling as she started to dial. "Lewis?"

"Hello, there."

"Look, I'm terribly sorry, tomorrow is out."

"Caroline—what are you trying to do to me?"

The receiver was wet and slippery in her hand. "I'm sorry, I just can't help it. Edward's brother and his girl friend have arrived almost out of the blue. I thought I could still get away for a while, but Edward's decided we should all go out for the day tomorrow, so there's no chance."

"How most inconsiderate of him!"

"Yes. However, we are having a few friends in for drinks at lunchtime on Sunday. Will you be able to come?"

"And gaze on you from afar like forbidden fruit? I'd hoped we were past that stage."

"Please, Lewis," she said with difficulty.

"All right, I'll be there. I must go. Harry's standing here with his tongue hanging out and it's nearly closing time! See you."

He rang off and she was left wondering rather uneasily just how much of the conversation Harry had overheard. Hurriedly she phoned Paul Denver, Tom and Patty Howard and two other couples. As she emerged from her room, Gillian was coming out on the landing, closing Laura's door behind her, and they went down the stairs together.

"They can all come," Caroline told them as she and Gillian rejoined the two brothers. "Lewis, Paul Denver, the Howards, the Freemans and the Lakes."

"Fine."

Richard reached out a hand to Gillian. "Come here, moon of my delight, and convince me that all is not lost!"

"And what does that mean?" she asked with a laugh, but she went across and he pulled her down onto his knee, twining the fingers of one hand into her shining, tattered hair. Caroline carefully looked away. She was convinced that this open display of affection was designed solely to embarrass her and she was determined not to let Richard know that it had succeeded.

"I rather think, if you'll excuse me, that I'll follow Laura's example and go up too. I didn't sleep well last night."

Edward looked up and she knew he was remembering, perhaps guiltily, the strained atmosphere that had been between them.

"I won't be long, darling. I'll be up just as soon as I've packed off these two lovebirds."

"Don't let us keep you. We're quite happy!" Richard said lazily, and with deliberation he turned Gillian's face toward him with one finger and began to kiss her with unhurried thoroughness.

Edward gave a snort of amusement.

"Good night," Caroline said stiffly, to no one in particular, and thankfully left them to it.

Everyone except Caroline seemed to enjoy the day out. At last the long, cool spring was warming into summer and Laura's sleeveless dress pitilessly exposed the thinness of her arms. Even Gillian had forsaken her brown shroud in favour of an ultra-brief, exotically coloured shift which had the effect of making her look like a precocious twelve-year-old. Caroline wondered how old she really was. With all that carefully understated but skilfully applied makeup it was impossible to guess. She could have been twenty as easily as thirty.

Richard, in brilliant pink shirt, skin-tight trousers and open sandals, looked impossibly handsome and Bohemian and set off amiably along the country lanes with Laura on one arm and Gillian on the other, leaving Caroline to bring up the rear with Edward and Peter. It was a warm, balmy day and the meadows were lush with late lambs and buttercups, but she refused to let them delight her. She should have been spending these hours of drugged sweetness with Lewis, and her longing for him had materialized into a dull, dragging ache inside her. She replied to the comments of husband and son with scant attention and longed impatiently for the day to be over.

Sunday dawned even hotter and Edward carried out the garden furniture, arranging small tables and chairs in groups along the terrace which ran down the side of the house outside the sitting-room's French windows.

Caroline listened to the joyful pealing of the church bells as she prepared the canapés beside Mrs. Baines, and was aware of a rising tide of excitement. Perhaps after all they might manage a moment or two alone. Laura, humming gaily, had already laid out crisps and dishes of nuts. There was a quiet, contented expectancy about her which helped to soothe away the extraordinary doubts that had been expressed on Friday evening. Her day out yesterday had washed her pale skin with its first touch of gold and her cheeks were flushed. She looks almost pretty again, Caroline thought with surprise.

Richard and Gillian didn't appear downstairs till after eleven. Caroline said briefly over her shoulder, "I'm afraid you're out of luck if you're looking for breakfast, but you can make some coffee if you like. I haven't time to stop now."

"Dear Caroline," Richard remarked in tones of mock-sadness. "So transparently disapproving!"

"Does it worry you?" she snapped.

"Not at all, fair sister; not at all!"

Mrs. Baines came back into the room. "Ready for your breakfast now, are you, Mr. Richard?"

Richard threw Caroline a glance of malicious delight. "I've just been told I'm not to have any, Bainsy, as a punishment for getting up late. But I'd love some coffee."

"The tray's ready for you to take in, Mrs. Baines," Caroline said rather loudly.

"It's all right." Gillian's quiet voice was in marked contrast. "I've already put the kettle on. I'll do it."

Furiously, Caroline felt they were all treating her like a spoilt, spiteful child. She maintained an angry silence while Gillian opened various cupboard doors in search of cups and saucers and Richard perched himself on a corner of the table and opened the Sunday paper. Then, the last of her preparations completed, she left the room and went to change.

After the first couple had arrived, the later arrivals, seeing the groups in the garden, walked along the terrace to join them without ringing at the front door. Consequently, Caroline was not aware that Lewis had arrived until she came out of the French windows to find him talking to Laura and Richard.

"Hello, Lewis," she said lightly. "I see I'm too late to introduce you to my brother-in-law."

"Yes, we sorted ourselves out. How are you, Caroline? You look very cool and elegant."

"Caroline's always cool and elegant!" Richard remarked, managing to rob the compliment of its value.

"Really?" Lewis murmured, his eyes full of amused disbelief, and she excused herself hastily to greet Tom and Patty Howard. But as she stood chatting and smiling with them, she was still listening closely to the continuing conversation behind her. Laura, she noted, was voluble and laughing, seeming more at ease than she had since her arrival over three weeks ago. No doubt Richard would now dismiss any doubts he might have had and feel quite justified in leaving her at Four Winds. Caroline was unlikely to be free of her after all.

Edward had apparently just joined them with a plate of savouries. She heard him say, "I came straight to you with these, Laura, I know they're your favourites!" and Laura exclaimed jubilantly, "Smoked salmon! Hallelujah!" Simultaneously, Caroline felt a sudden violent movement from Lewis immediately behind her, and the drink in her glass spilled down her dress.

Tom Howard caught her arm to steady her, and, with a murmur of concern, began to dab ineffectually at the stain with his handkerchief. Caroline brushed him aside with scant ceremony and spun round to see what had happened. Lewis's face was livid, a horrible, greenish pallor, and the others were anxiously enquiring what was wrong.

"Nothing—really—I'm so sorry. It's only my ankle. I twisted it the other day when I slipped off a ladder during the decorating. I must have put uneven pressure on it, that's all. Was that you I knocked, Caroline? I am terribly sorry."

She took his arm. "Are you sure you're all right? At least come and sit down and rest your ankle."

He let her lead him towards a chair. "Is Laura coming?

We were in the middle of—"

"I'm right here, Lewis."

Caroline glanced from one of them to the other with faint perplexity. As she helped Lewis down into the chair, his colour was beginning to come back, but his breathing was still fast and shallow.

"Can I get you a cold-water compress or anything?" She was reluctant now to relinquish her charge of him, but his eyes were on Laura and he answered her almost impatiently, "No, no, I told you it was nothing." And, as an afterthought, "Thanks."

"Laura, perhaps you'd pass some things round?" Caroline suggested, striving to steady her voice, but Lewis laid a hand quickly on the girl's arm.

"Not at the moment, please, Caroline."

With head high and eyes stormy she had no choice but to move away and leave them together. She almost cannoned into Paul Denver before she saw him, but she greeted him with more enthusiasm than she ever had before.

"Paul! Just the person I want! I have to keep moving about among my guests, but would you do something for me? Go and sit with Laura and keep an eye on her. I'm worried about her."

"Of course." He moved off with alacrity and Caroline forced herself to chat lightly to John and Philippa Lake. Philippa was one of her bridge friends from the Ledbrook Club and John occasionally played golf with Edward.

Philippa seized her arm effusively. "I was saying to Valerie only the other day that I haven't seen you for ages. We must fix up a four for bridge."

"I'd love to. Since Laura arrived, things have been a bit complicated."

"How is she now? She looks rather fragile. John was just remarking what an attractive little thing she is."

"You think so?" Caroline turned to John in surprise.

"Oh, certainly. A bit under par still, obviously, but that will-o'-the-wisp quality is irresistible, you know. Makes a man feel strong and protective!"

"Really?" said Caroline thoughtfully.

Pride kept her away from Lewis for the rest of the party, but from time to time her eyes went to him of their own accord. Each time, he was earnestly engaged in conversation with Laura, his eyes on her face with an odd, almost hungry intentness. Over their heads her eyes met Richard's, and he lifted his shoulders in a nonplussed shrug.

Caroline developed a raging headache. Nothing had worked out the way she had planned. Although it was ridiculous to be jealous of Laura of all people, there was no doubt that at the moment Lewis appeared to prefer her company to Caroline's, and Paul's stiff presence at the table had done nothing to interrupt their concentration on each other. Resolutely she kept on smiling, and at last people began to leave.

As Paul took her hand, she said quickly, "How does she seem to you?"

He shrugged. "It's hard to say. Bright—almost feverishly so." He gave a short laugh but she could tell that he was hurt. "Actually, she hardly seemed aware of my existence. Neither of them were." His eyes challenged her. "I didn't know anything about this book they're planning."

"It was only decided on the other day."

"If that's the effect it's going to have on her—" He broke off, flushing a little. "Anyway, it's none of my business. Thank you for a pleasant party, Mrs. Hardy. I'm sorry I wasn't more help to you." He moved away, leaving her to wonder if he had seen through her excuse in asking him to join them.

At nine-thirty that evening the telephone rang and Caroline, who happened to be passing, answered it.

"Caroline? Lewis."

Her hand tightened spasmodically on the receiver. "Yes?"

She heard him laugh. "Still on your high horse? Surely you agree it was better for us not to take too much notice of each other?"

Was that really all it had been, that engrossment with Laura? One gigantic playact to divert suspicion from his real interest in herself? The hard knot that had been inside her since lunchtime eased slightly.

"How's your ankle?"

"My what? Oh, that. Right as rain. Listen, officially I'm ringing like a dutiful guest to thank you for having me. What I really want to let you know is that I'll be at home all tomorrow afternoon. Any hope of you making it this time?"

Her heart began to slam against her ribs painfully. "I think I might. Richard and Gillian left this evening."

"Perhaps it will be third time lucky, then."

"Yes." Her mouth was dry. He did want her; of course he did. How could she have doubted him?

"As soon as you can," he urged softly.

"Yes," she said again. "Good-bye, Lewis."

Alone in the hall she spun a private little pirouette of sheer joy before moving sedately towards the sitting-room to join Edward in front of the television.

Chapter 7

CAROLINE was sleepy and warm and sub-
limely happy. The diamond-paned window was open and
on the branch of a tree just outside a wood-pigeon was
clucking and cooing to itself in the drowsy heat of the
summer afternoon. She turned contentedly on her side,
spread-eagling her hand on Lewis's chest.

"I love you," she murmured. "I love you, I love you!"

His hand came up to hers, tracing between each of her
outstretched fingers. After a moment she opened her eyes
and prompted gently, "Aren't you going to say you love
me too?"

He smiled a little. "If you want me to."

She stared at him for a moment and the first nebulous
doubts stirred in her mind—doubts which flung back at
her like a douche of cold water the sheer lunacy of her
abandonment to him, let alone that last, unguarded admis-
sion.

She tried to keep her voice level. "But it wouldn't be
true?"

He was still smiling. "Oh, come on, Caroline!"

"No, Lewis, I want to know." She propped herself up
on one elbow, staring down into his face.

"Then I put it to you," he said quietly after a moment,
"that all this love business is largely euphemistic. If you
feel that to say 'I love you' makes it all more excusable and
respectable, then okay, I'll say it. But let's be adult about
it."

"I see." She was profoundly hurt and seeming to sense this, he added more gently, "I enjoyed making love to you. I rather think you enjoyed it too. Isn't that enough?"

"Apparently it has to be," she said stiffly. Her humiliation burned in her throat and stung her eyes.

"Don't spoil it all, honey. Lord knows, we've had to wait long enough for this. Can't we just enjoy it without getting embroiled in definitions of love?"

He studied her face, but she refused to meet his eyes. "You know, it was your unapproachability that attracted me in the first place. I set myself a time limit to get through to you!"

She stiffened furiously but his arm reached up and pulled her against him, holding her with the inflexibility of an iron band. "Easy, girl, that was supposed to be a compliment! There aren't many women I'm prepared to wait that long for, but I have to admit you were worth it!"

"And did you land me within your time limit?" she enquired with icy sarcasm, and felt him smile.

"Just!"

She raised her head, her eyes stinging with furious tears. "You—you male chauvinist pig!"

He gave a brief laugh. "Look at it my way. You're a highly respectable and extremely attractive married woman with a good husband and a lovely home. But you're bored. Me, I'm an adequately successful journalist. I'm not married, but I'm bored too. If we can give each other a good time within the confines of our circumstances, well, who could ask for more? To my mind it's an ideal setup."

"Meaning I can't make any demands on you?" Her few tears had dried stiffly on her cheeks and she was fully in control again, listening with almost clinical detachment to his assessment of the situation which was so heart-stoppingly different from her own. What a fool she'd been to expect otherwise.

"I can't believe you'd want to. Oh, Caroline, I thought you were more worldly than this! Why do women always have to keep harping on love?"

She met his eyes at last. "Damn you!" she said softly. "Damn you to hell!"

"That's better!"

She moved away from his restraining grasp and flung herself over on her back, staring up at the low ceiling. He sat up and reached for cigarettes from the table by the bed, lit one, and leant over to put it between her lips. She drew in deep lungfuls of the soothing, aromatic smoke and gradually a measure of calm came to her.

"I used to think I was hard, but my God, you could teach me a thing or two!"

"Perhaps you haven't had as many knocks as I have."

"Do you never consider anyone but yourself?"

"Not if I can help it. Do you?"

She didn't reply directly. "Haven't you ever been in love yourself, if you'll pardon the expression?"

She thought he hadn't heard and turned her head to repeat the question when the expression on his face stopped her.

"Once," he said at last, and reached out to reclaim his cigarette.

"What happened?"

"She died."

"I'm sorry." She could sense his rigidity. "You weren't married, were you?"

"No, she was."

"I see." She couldn't resist adding, out of her own hurt,

"So although you were still playing by your own rules, that time you were hoist with your own petard!"

"Shut up!"

She swung her head towards him, startled at the venom in his voice, but before she could speak, he flung back the sheet and walked rapidly over to the window, leaning on the sill and staring down into the sun-dappled lane.

She said awkwardly, "Lewis, I'm sorry. I didn't realize it still hurt so much."

He was still staring out of the window. "It's these last months that have brought it all back. She used to love hearing all about Four Winds. 'Tell me about the dining-room,' she'd say, or 'Describe the hall again!' She wanted to build up a complete mental picture of it. I don't know why, perhaps because it was so much a part of me."

"But you never took her there?"

"No. It wasn't—feasible."

"If she hadn't died, might you ever—?"

"God knows!" he said harshly. The bleakness in his voice tore at her and she slipped off the bed and padded over to him. He turned towards her and they stood holding each other for some time. It was ironic, she thought, that she should be trying to comfort him on behalf of the unknown girl who had succeeded in gaining his love where she herself had so abysmally failed. The breeze from the open window playing on her bare shoulders began to chill her and she shivered a little. He held her out then at arm's length, and the banter was back in his eyes.

"Lovely, wanton Caroline!"

"I must go," she said softly, "it's getting late."

His lips moved over her hair. "Have I disappointed you, Caroline?"

Pride came to her rescue. "No, I hadn't formed any expectations, so I could hardly be disappointed, could I?"

"All the same, I fear my attitude may have left something to be desired. If so, I'm sorry, but there's little I can do about it. Am I forgiven?"

She smiled. "I suppose so."

"And you'll come again?"

"If I'm asked!"

"I promise you you will be!"

"By the way, Laura said—"

His face clouded. "Oh, yes. Laura."

She said quickly, "Lewis, if you've changed your mind, if you don't want her to write this infernal book, you've only to say so."

He shook his head. "No, she has to do it, whether I like it or not."

"That's nonsense!" she said sharply, disturbed by the mindless acceptance implicit in his words.

He moved suddenly, releasing her, and lit another cigarette while she dressed. At the foot of the steep wooden staircase he kissed her lingeringly.

"Good-bye, Lewis." Her eyes went over his face.

"Good-bye, sweet Caroline."

She pulled the door to behind her and started briskly back down the lane that led to Brocklehurst High Street. Well, she'd done it. For the first time in her married life she had been unfaithful to Edward, and her only regret in the whole, magical interlude was the fact that she had tried to make Lewis tell her he loved her. She could only hope that her subsequent nonchalance had convinced him that she too had been using the word euphemistically. But had she? Was this throbbing, tearing urgency that possessed her at the very thought of him nothing more than sheer physical need? Even if it were not, she must make herself believe so.

She turned left into the High Street as the hourly bus lumbered past. Five o'clock already. Peter would be home from school before long. By then, she knew, her everyday life would have taken hold of her again and these last precious hours with Lewis would seem like a dream.

The next morning, shortly before nine o'clock, Caroline was startled to find Lewis himself on the doorstep.

"I brought these books round for Laura," he told her. "There are a few notes, photographs, and so on. If she can find time to browse through them during the day, it'll be something to go on this evening."

She stared at him uncomprehendingly and the corner of his mouth lifted. "I—er—didn't seem to find time to mention it yesterday, but Edward and I discussed the pros and cons of this book of hers on Sunday. He doesn't seem to like the thought of her coming to the cottage, for which, in the circumstances, I can hardly blame him, so it's been arranged that we should spend a couple of hours here each evening until she has the framework clear. She'll tape the relevant bits and then write up her own notes the next day."

"You're—coming here every evening?"

"Will it disturb you?"

"Infinitely!"

"Good," he said softly. "It will disturb me too but there would appear to be no way round the problem. We'll do our best not to inconvenience you, ma'am!" He glanced past her into the hall, leant forward swiftly and kissed her mouth. "Till this evening, then!" He thrust the bundle of papers into her hands and got back into his car, turned it, and, after waiting a few minutes as the rush-hour traffic sped by, inched his way out of the gates with a wave of his hand.

Behind her Laura said eagerly, "Was that Lewis? Are those for me?" She flicked quickly through them and extracted a plain-backed scrapbook, dropping the other papers onto the monk's bench. Caroline watched her curiously as she rapidly turned the pages until, with an exclamation, she stopped at a blank page. In the middle of it was a splotch of ancient glue that had apparently once held something in position.

"He's taken it out!" Laura's voice rang with disappointment. "I wonder why ever he did that!"

"Taken what out?"

"Her photograph. It was here when I looked through the book at the cottage."

"Whose photograph, for heaven's sake?"

Laura looked up, as though aware for the first time that she had been speaking aloud, and a guarded look came over her face. "It doesn't matter," she said in a low voice.

Caroline looked at her helplessly. It seemed very likely that the photograph which had been removed from the album was of the girl Lewis had loved. Jealously, she wondered what Laura knew about her, but it was impossible to ask. She could only watch as, humming to herself, Laura gathered up the papers, flashed her an absent-minded smile, and retreated with them up the stairs to her room. Slowly Caroline returned to the vase of flowers she had been arranging.

The next two weeks were a time of increasing strain for Caroline. Her days were a prolonged waiting for Lewis's visits, but when he did come, she hardly saw him. He and Laura formed the habit of taking deck chairs across the garden by the fruit trees, where they were able to get the benefit of the last of the evening sunshine. From her usual chair in the sitting-room, Caroline could see them quite clearly, and many a time her eyes slipped sideways from the television screen to that other picture framed by the window of the man and girl laughing together under the tree. And there was a lot of laughter, she thought resentfully. She had never known either of them as relaxed as they seemed to be in each other's company now that the strangeness had gone.

"I thought you and Richard had decided Lewis wasn't good for Laura," she burst out angrily one evening. Edward turned to her in surprise.

"Well, you heard her reaction when he suggested she should go back with them."

"It might have been wiser not to allow her the choice," she replied in a clipped tone.

"Come, come, she's over twenty-one!"

"But apparently not old enough to know what's good for her. However, Laura wants to see him and that's good enough for you and Richard. She must always have what she wants."

Edward folded his paper resignedly. "Are we going to go through all that again?"

"You must admit it's not healthy for her to be so immersed in Lewis! You said yourself he must be at least twenty years older than she is. She's not seen anything of that Denver boy for weeks."

"That, at least, should please you," Edward remarked caustically.

"Actually it doesn't. I'd rather she saw him than Lewis."

"But why? I thought you liked Castleton?"

She drew a long, tremulous breath. "I do, but frankly

these daily visits are beginning to be a bit much. The house isn't our own any more. I can't relax. You know how I often have my bath about nine o'clock and come downstairs in my housecoat? I can hardly do that when he's liable to walk in at any minute!" She was not even aware of the irony of her complaint.

"I don't see why not," Edward returned reasonably. "It's not you he's coming to see. And anyway there's nothing wrong with your housecoat. As a matter of fact, I'm more concerned about you than about Laura at the moment. You're very tense, aren't you? Is she really getting you down to that extent?"

Her eyes strayed out of the window in time to see Lewis's dark head bent close to Laura's over a scrapbook. "Yes!" she said tightly.

He sighed. "I'm sorry, dear. I suppose I should have realized. Never mind, as soon as she's finished writing, she can go to Richard or Toby for a while. She could even type out the manuscript with them and give you a break." He paused. "Surely she's not all that much trouble though? She seems to spend most of her time in her room anyway. Why don't you put her out of your head occasionally and carry on as you did before she came? Phone Val or Philippa for a game of bridge or something."

"The panacea to all ills!"

"You don't seem prepared to make any effort to help yourself." Edward, losing interest, picked up his paper again.

She stood up. "I'm going for a bath. Perhaps that will help me to relax."

"And to hell with Lewis?"

"Exactly!"

She stayed in the bathroom a long time, creaming and

massaging her face, giving herself a manicure and finally settling down with a magazine in the hot, scented water. But though the physical strain slowly eased away, her mind was still locked on Lewis. When would he ask her to the cottage again? Had that unguarded mention of love given him second thoughts after all about the wisdom of continuing their association? It may well be, because if he really wanted to see her, surely he could spare a little time from the hours he spent here with Laura. Perhaps, she thought suddenly, the house itself was the magnet rather than Laura. What had he said about that girl wanting to hear about it? "Perhaps because it was so much a part of me." And that awoke another, less unpleasant echo in her mind. On the night he had been to dinner he had said about the "ghost child": "It's rather nice to think there's still a part of me here."

Caroline shivered suddenly, reached for the voluminous towel and stepped quickly out of the bath. She had schooled herself to forget all that nonsense. When they'd told Richard about it a fortnight ago, she had been almost frightened and she didn't intend to let it get hold of her again.

She stretched up to open the window. It was dark outside, the pulsating purple of summer night, star-sprinkled. Laura and Lewis must have come in by now. Caroline unlocked the door and had started back towards her bedroom when she stopped abruptly, her breath clogging in her throat. From behind Laura's closed door came the sound of low voices. With her heart hammering high in her breast, she moved a little closer in time to hear Lewis's voice say quietly, "Do you think you can understand how much it means to me?" and Laura's whispered reply, "Of course I do!"

He couldn't—he wouldn't dare! Scarcely aware of what she was doing, Caroline caught hold of the handle and wrenched the door open, rocking it violently back on its hinges. Laura's startled eyes flew to her face. She was sitting up in bed hugging her knees and on the table beside her was the cassette recorder. She leant over and switched it off, her eyes never leaving Caroline's. Then she said quietly, "Did you think he was here with me?"

Caroline's harsh breathing hurt her chest and rasped in her throat. "I'm sorry," she said at length. "I'd no right. Good night."

Laura's eyes, unreadable, were still steadily on her face. "Good night, Caroline."

It was two days later that Paul Denver phoned, and after a lot of low-voiced talk Laura eventually agreed to spend his free afternoon with him.

Caroline watched her go from the bedroom window. The temptation that had been with her ever since she burst into Laura's room could no longer be denied. Moving like a robot, trying not to think what she was doing, she crossed the landing to Laura's room, opened the door softly and closed it behind her.

The cassette recorder still lay on the bedside table. Caroline's mouth was dry. She sat on the bed and switched it on. Laura's voice, loud in the listening room, said clearly, ". . . the ormolu clock." Quickly Caroline turned down the volume. There was a pause while the tape went on turning, then Lewis's voice, jerky and strange: "How did you know about that?" "About what?" "The ormolu clock, for God's sake!" "I—I don't know. You must have told me." "I know for a fact that I didn't. There was only one person I told about that clock."

Caroline leant forward anxiously, afraid the tape had

110

broken in some way, but it was still winding on in another long silence. At last Lewis's voice came again, making her jump. "You know exactly what happened, don't you? That bloody crystal ball or whatever it is tells you everything about me!"

Caroline was gazing at the revolving cassette without breathing. Make it stop! she thought. I've heard more than enough! But she made no move to switch it off. She heard Laura start to reply and then suddenly, terrifyingly, a new voice cut in, a girl's voice which, in the initial moment of shock, reminded her in some way of Fenella Gray's.

"What are you trying to prove?" it demanded furiously. "This is no concern of yours!" As though pulled by strings, Caroline rose from the bed, staring down at the machine in fascinated horror. "Leave us alone, for God's sake, and be content with your husband!"

Caroline clasped her hands over her ears, her glazed eyes still on the suddenly hostile machine. Of its own accord the tape came to a sudden halt. Released at the same moment from her paralysis, Caroline rushed out of the room, down the stairs, out of the open French windows and across the garden, where she flung herself down under Lewis and Laura's tree and gave herself up to the terrified, tearless sobs that racked her shaking body.

Chapter 8

CAROLINE had been badly frightened by her experience with the tape, but gradually, as panic receded, she convinced herself that there must be a logical explanation. The fact that the words had seemed directed specifically at her was due to her own guilty conscience. It was the voice itself she couldn't explain—she hadn't known Lewis and Laura had met elsewhere with the tape, but they obviously must have done. "Leave *us* alone," it had said. Could it have been speaking to Laura? But she had no husband to be content with.

It was about a week later, when Laura had again given in to Paul's persistent invitation, that a ring at the doorbell roused Caroline from her sun-drenched dozing on the terrace.

Since it was Mrs. Baines's day off, there was no help but to answer it herself. She thrust bare feet into thonged sandals and went through the hall to the door. Lewis was standing there, and at the sight of him a wave of weakness flooded over her and she put a hand on the lintel for support.

"Hello, Lewis."

"Good afternoon. I've brought a few photos that Laura wanted."

"I'm afraid she isn't in." She paused, her eyes on him. "In fact, no one is, except me."

His eyes held hers and she watched them change, become aware of her.

"How very fortunate," he said softly.

"Would you—like to come in?"

"I should indeed."

She stepped aside, trembling as he brushed past her into the hall. Now that at last she was alone with him, she was flustered, unsure of herself.

"I was sunbathing."

"So I see." He followed her as she led the way into the sitting-room.

"Can I get you a cold drink?"

"No, thank you."

She hesitated, searching for something to say, and he gave a low laugh. "Come here!"

She lifted her head to meet his eyes but made no move towards him.

"Defiance?" He smiled. "Then the mountain will come to Mohammed!" With a quick stride he reached her, his hands moving over her bare back and shoulders, his mouth closing on hers as she strained feverishly against him.

"God!" he said shakily. "It's been a long time—too long. I can't imagine why I—" He broke off and turned his head sharply.

"What's the matter?" Her lips moved caressingly over his cheekbone and jaw.

"I thought I heard something."

"There's no one here, I assure you. Oh, Lewis!"

His mouth came back to hers, but a moment later he broke away again.

"Darling, what *is* it?"

"I'm not sure." He gave a short laugh. "You know, I always have the most damnable feeling in this house that someone is watching my every move. You don't go in for two-way mirrors, I presume?"

"That wasn't one of the mod cons we put in, no. But if you'd prefer it, we could go upstairs?" That, surely, was what he was angling for?

"An excellent solution! Clever Caroline!" He caught hold of her hand and they went together up the wide staircase. Around them the old house lay passive, listening. On the landing a board creaked suddenly and Lewis stopped, his hand tightening on hers.

"Look, on second thoughts we might be taking rather a risk."

"Nonsense!" she said quickly. "Laura's out with Paul and it's Mrs. Baines's half-day. No one will be back for hours. Relax, darling!"

She slipped her hand from his and pushed open the bedroom door. A trembling impatience took hold of her as she bent to fold back the counterpane.

"Oh, Lewis, I was really beginning to wonder—"

Suddenly aware that he hadn't followed her, she turned quickly. He was standing in the doorway, a strange, embarrassed expression on his face.

"Caroline—" His eyes fell away from hers. "Look, I know it seems ridiculous, but—I can't. Not here."

"What on earth are you talking about?" Her voice was unbecomingly shrill.

"I don't know what the hell it is, but his house inhibits me. The clinging strands of my childhood, perhaps."

"But, Lewis, it's the first chance we've had for ages!" She had no pride left, only her desperate need of him.

"Do you think I don't know?" His voice was jagged. "God, I want it too, you know that. But not here." He gave a helpless shrug. "Sweetheart, I'm really terribly sorry—"

"Think nothing of it." She turned and walked to the window, hugging herself tightly with both arms to stay the trembling.

"I'd take you back to the cottage with me now, but I'm on my way to an appointment. I had half an hour in hand, that was all."

"I said it doesn't matter."

There was a brief, taut silence, then he said awkwardly, "Perhaps you'd like me to go, then."

"Please."

He waited but she didn't turn, didn't even move, and a moment later she heard his footsteps going back down the stairs. The front door opened and she stared stonily down as he came into sight, walking rapidly to his waiting car. Only then did the tears of frustration and bitter humiliation well up in her eyes. The house, the house, always the blasted house. If he loved it so much, how could it make him feel uncomfortable? There wouldn't be another opportunity like this. They had had the place to themselves and now, stupidly, pointlessly, she was left alone. Or was she? The numbing uncertainty which flitted without warning into her mind raised the hairs on her scalp in prickling slow motion and she felt the goose flesh shiver on her bare arms.

Suddenly, overwhelmingly, she was conscious of a feeling of deep resentment directed specifically against herself, as though her presence here was an intrusion, as though she and the house had been engaged in some silent struggle to claim Lewis, and the house had won.

Almost fearfully she moved her head slowly from side to side, but the scene which met her apprehensive eyes was no different from at any other time. The only thing out of place was the hastily turned-back counterpane, and

115

as she caught sight of it, her breath twisted in a hard, choking sob.

"Well, are you satisfied?" she flung at the empty room. The door swung shut on a tiny, answering click, and she bit back a cry. Ridiculous—Lewis hadn't shut it properly, that was all. But what had Edward said about Laura being afraid to enter that first day? And there had been that uncanny business with the tape. Could there after all be something in all these unaccountable happenings?

She straightened, fighting to control her racing breath. Imagination. Of course it was. And she had resolved not to give in to it. If she could explain to her own satisfaction the mystery voice on the tape, that would be one step in the right direction. In fact, that was the only concrete fact in the whole ludicrous case she had built up.

Before she had a chance to change her mind, she ran across to Laura's room. Since some days had passed, a new cassette was in the machine. Ignoring the ethics of her actions, Caroline tugged open the drawer of the bedside table. Sure enough, the completed cassette lay inside. Swiftly she slipped it into the machine and played it back till she judged it was the part she had heard before. Laura's voice said suddenly, "I was up to date with the notes by lunchtime, so I thought I might as well start on the actual appearance of the house as you knew it. You'd described it so well I could almost see it, anyway, the horsehair sofa in the sitting-room, the turkey-red carpet and the high mantelpiece with the ormolu clock." The tape whirred on for a while before Lewis's sharp query: "How did you know about that?" and then Laura saying she thought he must have told her and his denying it. Now, this was the part she wanted—

Caroline leant forward intently, hands tightly clasped.

116

This time she wouldn't panic and run away like a fool, she'd play it over and over until she could understand how those particular sentences had come into the context about the clock.

"—crystal ball or whatever it is tells you everything about me!"

Laura's voice said hesitantly, "Lewis—please don't be angry. I only thought—well, even if you didn't actually mention it, it was just the setting for a—"

Caroline frowned, chewing on her lip. Surely it was here that—? She let the machine run on for a few minutes and then stop as it came to the end of the tape. There was no trace whatsoever of the voice that had disturbed her so much. Puzzled, she flicked the switch and played the passage through again. Definitely this was what she had listened to before. The intruding voice couldn't have been erased, because while it had been speaking, she'd been aware of Laura's voice faintly in the background, replying to Lewis's accusation. Now it was simply that without the overriding sentences she could hear her more clearly.

Baffled and uneasy, Caroline went through the relevant portion once more before, defeated, she returned the cassette to the drawer and replaced the one which had been in the machine before.

Perhaps, she thought uncomfortably, the voice had been in her own head all the time, that of the conscience she had been trying to ignore over the last few weeks. But why, for heaven's sake, the American accent?

She shivered and stood up, suddenly cold. The house was cool after the heat outside and she was still in her brief sundress. She hurried out of Laura's room and back to the deck-chair she had left to answer Lewis's ring. It wasn't until she lay back in it, letting the hot canvas warm

117

her cool shoulders, that another uncomfortable thought came to her. She had not after all been able to prove anything with the tape. The house had won again.

Fortunately Caroline had accepted an invitation to play bridge that evening, and she was careful to leave the house before Lewis arrived for his two-hour session with Laura. Three times now he had rebuffed her, she reminded herself bitterly. On each occasion she had vowed he would not have another opportunity, and each time her treacherous body had betrayed her. She had no intention of laying herself open to any further fiasco. Yet even as she assured herself of this, she knew despairingly that she, who had always been so much in control of herself and everyone else, was powerless when it came to this one man. If he invited her again, as he surely would, she knew that she would go to him, and the knowledge in her present state of furious hurt was galling indeed.

She was soon put to the test; he phoned the next morning.

"Caroline, I feel all sorts of a fool about yesterday! I can't imagine what got into me—I must have been out of my mind! Ever since I left you I've been kicking myself. I won't be surprised if you tell me to go to hell, but I very much hope you won't."

He waited but she didn't, couldn't speak.

"Will you give me another chance? Please? I have to go to Tonbridge this morning but I'll be back about four. Will you come?"

She moistened her lips. "Lewis, I really think—"

"Look, I was a bloody fool and I hurt you, I know, but I have to see you. If you want me to beg, all right, I'm begging!"

For a moment longer she fought with herself, but she

knew it was useless. She heard herself say expressionlessly, "Very well, Lewis, I'll come."

It was very hot, close with the approach of thunder. Her hair was damp in the nape of her neck, clinging in little tendrils to the side of her face. The sun had disappeared and the light filtering into the room through the heavy branches of the tree outside filled it with a luminous green twilight.

She pulled deeply on her cigarette and moved her head lazily to look at him. "How's the book coming along?"

"All right, I believe. I haven't seen it."

"It's good of you to give up so much time to her." She hoped belatedly that the latent jealousy in the remark hadn't sounded as obvious to him as it had to her.

"I don't mind. You know, it's funny, but I enjoy being with her. She's a strange little thing."

"I shouldn't have thought she was your type," Caroline said acidly.

"That's just it, she's not. And yet—" He gave an embarrassed laugh. "Hell, you're the last person I should be discussing it with!"

"I don't see why. You made it very clear there are no strings. What were you going to say?"

He took the cigarette from her hand and drew on it himself, his eyes narrowed against the smoke. "It's hard to explain, but there's some curious kind of affinity between us, and it's getting stronger."

"I see."

"I think the root of it is that she reminds me of someone. God knows way—she looks nothing like her."

Caroline's nails bit into her palms. "The girl you once loved?"

119

He nodded almost absently, his eyes intent on the ceiling.

"It was her photograph you removed from the scrapbook?" she persisted.

"Yes. Stupid, I know, I just didn't want it to go out of the house."

"Go on." She was determined to sound cool and detached, to give no inkling of the frighteningly powerful jealousy that was tormenting her.

He said awkwardly, "You don't want to hear all this."

"But I do. Funnily enough, Richard said the same thing, about there being some kind of bond between you and Laura."

"Richard? Then I'm more surprised than ever that they agreed to let her go ahead with the book."

"I don't think they'd any choice. She was so intent on it there was no stopping her. Actually, Richard did try to make her agree to go back to London with him that weekend, but we all knew it was hopeless. Anyway, it was Edward who'd mentioned you first as someone who had seen a lot of—"

"Violence?" Lewis asked softly.

"Yes."

"A charming reputation to have, but true as far as it goes."

Caroline drew a deep breath. "Have there been any more instances of her 'remembering' things?"

He turned his head and looked at her oddly. "How do you mean?"

"Well, like the twisted trees, or that fairy tale about the little boy."

"Yes, there have, actually. Several."

"That reminds me, *did* you by any chance save Harry

Tait's life in Biafra?"

She felt his body tense. "How the hell—?"

"Laura told me."

"Well, I sure as hellfire didn't tell *her*. You know, Caroline, there are times when she puts the fear of God into me, and I vow I'm never going near her again. And then—I don't know. A sudden turn of her head or an intonation in her voice reminds me of Noel, and for that I'd follow her to the ends of the earth."

After a moment Caroline said tonelessly, "But you say she doesn't look like her."

"No. Yet sometimes I'd swear, if I shut my eyes, that it was Noel talking to me. She even uses some of her favourite expressions. The first time I noticed it was when we were having drinks that Sunday. That was what shook me, nothing to do with my ankle."

Caroline said slowly, "You know, she *is* different. Of course, when she first came out of hospital we expected her to be—well, subdued, but as she's grown stronger, it doesn't seem to be her own personality that she's reverted to. Not as she was before the accident, anyway. And she's developed an odd way of talking."

"So it's not just my imagination." There was a note in his voice which lifted the tiny golden hairs along her arms. "Odd in what way, would you say?"

"Just—unusual, somehow. This morning, for instance, she came into the dining-room winding her watch and said, 'What time do you have?' It sounded—wrong."

Lewis said very softly, "You mean she uses American phrases?"

"American? Yes. Of course, that's it! Because she hasn't an accent it didn't register, but that's it all right." She laughed a little. "Perhaps she's just been watching too much TV!"

Beside her Lewis lay unmoving. At last he said, "Is there anything else you can think of?"

"Not offhand, except for the endless humming. Sometimes I could scream. And it's always the same tune."

Lewis's hand snaked out and closed over hers, tightening remorselessly until she thought the bones would splinter.

"Lewis! Don't! Stop it—you're hurting me!"

"What tune?"

"What?"

"What is the tune she hums?"

"Hell, I don't know." She rubbed her bruised hand. "That thing that was very popular a few years ago— someone and his something brass. I used to like it, but I've heard enough of it this last couple of weeks to put me off for good."

"Hum it!" he commanded harshly.

"Lewis, what on earth—"

"Hum it, Caroline."

Hesitantly she hummed the first few bars and the words came back to her. "This guy's in love with you—"

With a suddenness that made her jump he swung his legs to the floor, sitting on the edge of the bed with his head in his hands while his rasping breaths grated through the eerie greenness of the room.

She said sharply, "Are you ill? Lewis—shall I get a doctor?"

He turned his head slowly and she was shocked at the expression on his face. "It's not a doctor we need," he said with difficulty. "If you ask me, it's bell, book and candle."

She stared at him with wide, frightened eyes. "I don't understand."

"That makes two of us."

"That tune—"

"It was Noel's favourite. We were dancing to it the first time I told her how I felt." His breathing was still laboured. "After that she bought the record and we played it every time we were together. Whenever I hear it, things come flooding back—odd incidental little details I'd forgotten. And Laura has the same effect. Simply by looking at her, I remember things that happened years ago, things I'd forgotten."

"Like the clock?" She was too distraught now, too caught up in his agitation, to care if she gave away her eavesdropping, and he too distraught to notice.

"Yes, that damnable clock. That was another instance. It had stood for years on the sitting-room mantelpiece; my mother was extremely proud of it. One day when she had punished me for something, I went in there. I suppose I must have been about eight or nine. Anyway, I had to stand on a stool to reach the mantelpiece. I simply and deliberately swept my hand along the length of it, and of course the clock fell into the fireplace and smashed in pieces. I can see it now, lying shattered with its innards whirring and coiling." He smiled thinly. "As you can imagine, it's not a memory I'm especially proud of. The only person I ever mentioned it to was Noel, who wanted to know all there was to know."

"And who has remembered," whispered Caroline.

His mouth twisted. "The same thing struck you?"

"She was American, wasn't she, Lewis?"

"She was indeed."

Not Fenella Gray after all. She shivered uncontrollably. "Leave us alone!" "Us"? Could that mean *Laura* and Lewis? But Laura wasn't Noel—was she?

She said on a high note, "Lewis, I'm frightened!"

"So am I, Caroline. So am I."

"We must do something to stop it!"

"No!"

"But, Lewis, it's—it's horrible!"

"Not horrible. Frightening, certainly, but not horrible."

"Does Laura know, do you think?"

"I've no idea what Laura knows."

"Edward will know what we should do."

"I said no! Nothing must be done to interrupt the sequence." He straightened at last and turned to her, his eyes burning in his livid face. "I forbid you to say anything to anyone, do you hear? Anyway, there's nothing concrete. It could all be imagination. This premature gloom doesn't help." He switched on the light and they blinked in its hard brilliance.

"But I must tell him, Lewis! She's going insane!"

"Nonsense. She's entirely rational. The most obvious explanation is that she's being used, perhaps without her knowledge, as some kind of medium. And you don't go putting them in padded cells, do you?"

"But surely we ought—"

"Caroline!" His voice lashed out at her and she came to an abrupt halt. "I lost her once. No one's going to make me lose her again!"

She said jerkily, "You're the one who's insane!"

"Perhaps. Heaven knows, it wouldn't be surprising if I were. But in the meantime you're to say *nothing* to anyone about this. I should only deny it anyway, and perhaps you'd be the one ending up with a psychiatrist!"

"This is the end, isn't it?" Her voice was shaking. "We can't go on after this."

"I don't know. God, I don't know *anything!* Caroline,

124

I'm sorry! It's not as though I can control it. You saw how it was at Four Winds."

She stared at him, her face white. "You mean it was *Noel* that—? My God, you *are* mad!"

"Can you honestly tell me you don't feel anything in that house?"

Against her will she remembered the impression she had received of the house pitting itself against her, the uncomfortable awareness of a malevolence, a kind of spite towards herself. Jealousy?

A sudden crash of thunder sounded directly overhead and the light flickered as lightning sliced through the room. At the same instant rain started to fall, drumming on the leaves of the tree outside and turning the approach lane into a sea of mud in seconds.

Caroline said shakily, "That tree's too close for comfort!"

"It's all right, we're in a dip here. Plenty of higher landmarks for it to strike."

The violent interruption of the storm was welcomed by both of them. Lewis said matter-of-factly, "One thing's sure, you can't go home in this."

"Could I have a shower, then?"

"Of course. I'll come down with you and put the kettle on for a cuppa too."

By the time she emerged from the bathroom extension, he had laid mugs on the kitchen table together with a packet of sugar and a bottle of milk.

"Afternoon tea at the Ritz!" Lewis said with a grin. "Help yourself. I'll have a quick shower too and get dressed." He gestured down at his dressing-gown. "The Noel Coward image is hardly me!"

She sat down and poured milk into the mugs. The

kitchen window looked out at the back of the cottage, a drenched jungle of overgrown grass and bushes, with the straggling outskirts of Gillet's Wood apparently only kept at bay by the broken-down fence.

She wouldn't come here again. She knew it, and so did Lewis. Their brief, tempestuous affair was over. Perhaps it was as well, since she was incapable of finishing it herself, that it had ended this way.

After a while he joined her, reaching out for his mug. "It's still bucketing down. Where are you supposed to have been this afternoon?"

"Shopping in Ledbrook."

"Then I'll say I found you sheltering from the rain and ran you home. As long as no one happens to see which direction the car comes from, that should cover us."

"You might as well stay for an evening meal, since you'd only have to come back again to see Laura. You won't be able to sit under your tree today."

He leant over, took up her hand and kissed the palm.

"What's that for?"

"Just to say thank you."

"And—good-bye?"

"In one sense, yes. I've behaved very badly, I know. I haven't hurt you too much, have I?"

"No," she answered steadily. "You never pretended it would last."

"We can still be friends?"

"We'll have to be, won't we, if you continue to see Laura?"

"Yes." The abstraction was back in his face and quite suddenly she had had enough. She scraped her chair back.

"Will you take me now? It's almost six. Peter will wonder what's delayed me."

"Of course. You'd better put my jacket over your head and make a run for the car. I'm afraid I don't possess an umbrella. I'll go first and open the door."

Edward was in the hall when they arrived, shaking the rain from his jacket. "Lord, what a day! Hello, Lewis. Did you rescue Caro? That's very good of you. Come and have a drink. Good heavens, let's have a bit of light on the subject. It's like the dead of night in here!"

Caroline said steadily, "I've asked Lewis to stay and eat with us, to save his coming back later. I'll just go and tell Mrs. Baines we'll be one extra for dinner."

"Fine. If you'll excuse me, I'll run up and change. I'm drenched! Pour yourself a drink, Lewis. I shan't be a moment."

Peter came hurtling down the stairs. "Where were you, Mum?"

She ruffled his hair. "Sheltering from the rain, silly!"

"I haven't any homework today!"

"Lucky you!"

She was behaving admirably, she told herself, not at all like a woman who has had to bow gracefully out of a relationship she would much rather have continued. It would take time, nevertheless, to school her body to ignore Lewis Castleton.

She left Peter helping Mrs. Baines arrange cheese biscuits on a plate and went back to the sitting-room.

"It won't be—" She broke off. Lewis and Laura were standing close together in the centre of the room, her face lifted to him with a radiancy which made Caroline catch her breath. With a choked murmur which neither of them heard, she retreated and closed the door softly behind her.

127

PART 3

Lewis

Chapter 9

WHEN Lewis returned to the cottage that evening, the mugs were still on the kitchen table and the milk in the bottle had turned, pervading the small room with its rancid odour. He poured it down the sink, watching the yellow globules separate and splay out against the white porcelain.

He rinsed the bottle, waiting until the water ran hot enough to remove the clogging cream round the neck, and then the two mugs. Now there was no reminder of Caroline but the rumpled bed upstairs. God, what a day!

He moved a hand over his forehead, pushing back the thick damp hair. The rain hadn't made it any cooler. He switched on the transistor, half-listening to the aimless patter of the disc jockey as he took a can of beer from the fridge and poured it into a glass. Then he hitched himself onto a corner of the table and fumbled in his pocket for cigarettes. His fingers, he noted dispassionately, were stained with nicotine. What the hell? If it killed him, he didn't care. His eyes returned broodingly to the upturned mugs on the draining board. Here, away from Four Winds and its tentacles, the idiocy of allowing the affair with Caroline to finish struck him forcibly for the first time. Of all the damn-fool things to do, especially when she was obviously anxious for it to continue. How could he possibly have let that pale, slip of a girl come between him and voluptuous, passionate Caroline?

He moved impatiently, drank deeply from his glass and

wiped his mouth with the back of his hand. The rain was still drumming relentlessly on the corrugated steel roof of the bathroom extension, and he felt as though it were beating on exposed nerves.

Restlessly he moved through to the living room, quite attractive now with the scattered rugs on its stained boards and the couple of easy chairs he had managed to pick up. He went over to the massive desk he had come across in a junk shop and which took up far more than its share of the small room. He unlocked it and as he pulled down the flap, his eyes fell on the photograph he had removed from the scrapbook. Incredibly, it was the only one he had of her. They had both been too cautious to use cameras.

Involuntarily his hand went out to pick it up, his eyes travelling millimetre by millimetre over the face that looked back at him, so intently that the image itself blurred in the minute, speckled detail of the paper on which it was printed.

The old, desperate sense of loss raged inside him. "I found this," she had said, reaching into her purse. He paused on the word, smiling even in his agony. Was that what Laura called her handbag now? "I thought you might like it. I won't write on it or anything. It's better not, but you know what I'd write if I could, don't you? 'This gal's in love with you!' "

They had been in that little hamburger bar in downtown New York, but even so she was wearing the dark glasses she always insisted on when they were out together.

"It makes me feel I'm going around with Greta Garbo!" he'd teased her.

"But you do understand, darling?" she'd pleaded. "If there was ever any hint—"

"Oh, I understand!" He hadn't troubled to hide his bitterness, even though he knew that it hurt her. "We must never take any risks that might upset your precious husband, must we? What does it matter if we happen to be tearing ourselves apart, as long as he's all right?"

"Lew!" Her face was white, but he couldn't see her eyes through the damn glasses. "Honey, I did warn you, right from the first."

"Oh yes, I was lucky to make even first base with you, wasn't I? What was it they called you? The chaste, the untouchable Mrs.—"

"Hush!" Frantically she leant forward and laid a finger on his mouth and he caught hold of it with a reassuring pressure.

"All right, I know. I'm sorry."

"I never meant this to happen," she went on tremulously. "You see, it's what he's always been afraid of, that I'd find someone—"

"Younger?" he interrupted brutally.

After a moment she said in a low voice, "It would be like throwing his age in his face."

"But he promised to release you! All you have to do is ask!"

She smiled a little. "Like Soames and Irene? But it didn't work out for them, either."

His eyes refocussed on the photograph—the sweet curving mouth, the broad brow and wide, trusting eyes. What had he done to her? What had they done to each other?

He waited, holding his breath, for the pain to reach the unbearable crescendo as it always did when he allowed his thoughts to go back unchecked. Incredibly, this time it didn't come. Instead, like a balm to his tortured soul, came the thought of Laura, peacefully sleeping at Four

133

Winds. Slowly his fingers unflexed and he relaxed.

Gently he replaced the photograph, locked up the desk and began to prepare for bed. He couldn't begin to understand the permutations which flickered in his mind, seeming one moment to offer a plausible solution but dissolving before he could grasp and understand them. Slowly, with his head still full of unanswerable questions, he went up the narrow wooden staircase to bed.

The next morning the rain had gone and grass and leaves glowed with renewed greenness. Lewis awoke with the sun on his face and a feeling of happy expectancy. He had intended driving down to the south coast today in connection with a series he was contemplating on British seaside resorts. There could hardly be a better day on which to put the plan into effect and, he thought on a rising tide of excitement, he could call in at Four Winds on the way and see if Laura would like to go with him.

She and Caroline were still at breakfast when he arrived, shortly before nine. Caroline was pale and composed, courteously pouring him a cup of coffee as he rather self-consciously put forward his proposal, but Laura was delighted at the prospect of the unexpected outing.

"Oh, Lewis, I'd love to!" She turned to her sister-in-law. "It would be all right, wouldn't it, Caroline? You haven't made any other arrangements?"

"No, nothing, but I hope the long drive won't tire you."

"I'm sure it won't!" Laura pushed back her chair. "Can you wait just a moment while I get a cardigan? It might be cooler coming home." She ran out of the room and his eyes met Caroline's.

"You do understand—" he began awkwardly.

"My dear Lewis, if you're going to apologize every time

we meet, we'll never get back on a normal footing!" She stood up suddenly. "Will you excuse me? I have a meeting in Tonbridge at ten—it's time I was going."

"Of course." He stood while she left the room and then pulled out his chair again to finish his cup of coffee.

"And did you really have a stag's head on the dining-room wall?" Noel had demanded delightedly. "I thought that was only in the stately homes!"

"Not at all," he'd replied smilingly, "many lesser homes had them, I assure you, Four Winds among them."

"Didn't you use to run into the hall to see where the rest of it was?"

It was a moment before he realized that it was Laura, and not his memory of Noel, who had spoken.

"What?" He stared at her blankly.

"Sorry—I thought—I mean—weren't you thinking of the old stag's head? You were staring at the wall just where you said it used to be."

"Yes, of course. You're quite right, as always." He took her arm and felt her tremble slightly, as she had in the sitting-room the previous evening. His eyes as he looked down at her were oddly tender. "Will you be warm enough?"

"Yes, I'll be fine."

It was a glorious drive through some of England's most beautiful countryside—fields of hops, white-washed cottages and the quaint, bent roofs of oasthouses. Laura said musingly, "You know, I was terribly disappointed the first time I saw Brocklehurst. I guess I hadn't really wanted to come at all, though it sounds ungrateful to admit it, but I'd at least hoped for a pretty village like some of these we're passing through."

"I suppose Brocklehurst hasn't much claim to beauty.

I've never really thought about it. It was just home, that's all. I know every inch of the woods and lanes round about. We used to picnic in them, and collect birds' eggs and play all sorts of wild games, and then later, when we grew up a bit, we'd walk with our girl friends there."

"You and Barry and Dave?"

"That's right."

After a moment she said hesitantly, "You—did tell me about them, didn't you?"

"Of course." And he saw that the worried crease had left her brow.

"We had a letter from Fenella this morning," she told him a little later.

"Who's Fenella?"

"I was forgetting. You never met her, did you? She was poor Mr. Sandilands' assistant."

"Ah. Yes. And how is she?"

"Writing steadily, she says. The book should meet the publication deadline despite everything. She was asking how *my* study on violence was progressing."

"What shall you tell her?"

She laughed. "Well, we have digressed a bit, haven't we? The only violence we've touched on so far is the smashing of the ormolu clock!"

"True. Unfortunately my intention of fighting as a mercenary in the Spanish Civil War never came to anything. Possibly it had something to do with the fact that I was only nine at the time!"

She smiled. "What was your first brush with violence, then?"

"National Service, I suppose, directly after the war. I don't know whether that gave me a taste for adventure, but it certainly awoke my wanderlust. Anyway, aren't

136

you rather jumping the gun? We've some way to go yet before we reach that epoch."

"What was the war like? It seems incredible to think how it must have been, with the Battle of Britain being fought almost directly overhead on beautiful summer days like this."

"It was pretty grim then, but at least we had no bombing round us. There was a constant fear of invasion, of course, to begin with, but after that faded, the thing that stands out most clearly in my mind is sweet-rationing!"

"But you remember the German pilot, surely?" She stopped, her eyes dilating, but he said smoothly against the jerk of his heart,

"Of course. He crashed in a field just outside Ledbrook. The all-clear had gone by then and we all got our bikes out and cycled hell for leather down the lanes to find out what the almighty bang had been. He'd bailed out, of course, and we arrived as he was being escorted from the field by the police. I can see him now, not much more than a boy, with close-cropped fair hair and a white, frightened face. You know, I think that was the first time it dawned on me that Germans were actually human."

There was a short silence, then she said quietly, "Thank you."

"For what?"

"For pretending you'd already told me about it when you hadn't. Do I ever frighten you, Lewis? I frighten myself quite often nowadays. It's strange the way it's all snowballed. At first, you know, I didn't like you at all, but ever since that night you came to dinner, I seem to have been drawn to you more and more."

"I know," he said gently.

"It happened gradually, though. For a while I only liked

137

you when we were both at Four Winds. Isn't that ridiculous? As though it's possible to like someone in one place and not another."

"And do I improve on acquaintance?" he asked humorously, but despite his light tone he was tense as he waited for her reply.

"Either that or the influence is getting stronger."

The car swerved under his hands. "What influence, Laura?"

She glanced at him in surprise. "I thought you knew."

"Tell me anyway." But after a moment she shook her head.

"It doesn't matter."

He didn't press the point, but the wild surmises which had plagued him in the night were back in his head like a swarm of buzzing flies.

By the time they reached Eastbourne, a stiff breeze was blowing off the sea and they were glad to leave the close confines of the car. She went with him into the small cafés and big hotels, into the cheap souvenir shops and ice-cream parlours, listening while he asked questions and jotted down the answers in his own personal shorthand.

They had lunch in an imposing hotel dining-room amid a crowd of happy, sunburned holiday-makers. Lewis watched Laura while she watched their fellow diners. Beside Caroline she had always seemed pale and colourless, but here, in her own right, as it were, he saw that he had underrated her. The silver-blonde hair had an ethereal quality, and although the sun had touched her skin to a pale honey, the blue veins were still clearly visible beneath the surface. There was a kind of fragile delicacy about her which, to his surprise, awoke in him a fierce protectiveness.

138

"What did you mean," he asked before he could stop himself, "about the influence getting stronger?"

She turned back to him and answered calmly, "Only that at first she could only reach you at Four Winds. You must have described it for her so well that she was quite at home there. Those twisted trees, the first day I arrived, they were what she would have expected to see, weren't they?"

He gazed at her, dumbfounded by the explicitness of her explanation. "You don't mind?"

"Not now. She was so desperately unhappy. I was aware of it all the time. Now that I'm doing what she wants, she's much happier."

"What does she want?" He wondered briefly, crazily, how this conversation would sound to Edward, even to Caroline.

"Only to be near you again. It was really very clever, the way she arranged things, making me want to write about violence—perhaps even putting pressure on Edward to suggest you as a guide. How he'd resent that! Of course, it was really only an excuse for me to be with you, to find out everything I could about you, for her."

"Couldn't she have found out for herself?"

"No, she couldn't reach you directly. I think she must have been trying all the time. By the time I arrived at Four Winds she was desperate. She latched onto me straightaway and luckily for her, this time it paid off. I've no idea why. Perhaps I'm what's known as a 'sensitive.' " She smiled a little. "She's very determined, I suppose you know that. She gave me no peace until I accepted her."

He leant across the table towards her. "Laura, what about you in all this?"

"I?" She looked bewildered.

"Mightn't it get rather out of control?"

"No, of course not. She won't need me much longer. She's in touch with you again and because of me she's able to move about more freely now. She doesn't have to wait until you visit Four Winds."

"But—surely it's rather more than that. She—actually *speaks* through you sometimes, doesn't she?"

She frowned. "I don't know what you mean."

He stared at her with mounting disquiet. So after all she didn't realize the full extent of Noel's power. For it was hardly likely that Noel, whose forceful personality had already made use of Laura's frail, compliant body, would ever be content to let her go, to be merely a spirit again without a body to enter at will.

He said harshly, "You're playing with fire, you must realize that."

"I hadn't much choice. Shall I tell you something else? I dreamt about you before I met you that day at the Howards' party. You called me—Noel."

It was the first time she had spoken the name and he saw the ripple that passed over her face. He had an absurd impulse to cross himself—he, to whom the name of God was no more than a convenient oath. Instead, he said softly, "You're very brave, Laura. Thank you, from both of us."

It was almost laughable, he thought distractedly, that this conversation, more suited to a churchyard at dead of night, should be taking place in the relaxed, midday sunshine of a holiday hotel. Bell, book and candle. He shuddered, wrenched his attention back to the waiter and called for their bill.

It was after six when they left Eastbourne and they stopped at a small roadside hotel for dinner an hour later.

140

"Do you intend to carry on the farce of writing my memoirs?" he enquired idly over coffee.

"Oh, it's not a farce. I didn't mean to imply that. After all, I am supposed to be a writer and we've put a lot of hard work into it already. It's extremely interesting and anyway, Edward would never forgive me if I backed out now!"

Lewis said reflectively, "On the contrary, I think he would probably be vastly relieved."

"Why?"

"Didn't he and Richard try to persuade you to go back to London to get away from me?"

"Oh, they've got over that by now."

"Do you get on well with Edward—and Caroline?"

She hesitated. "They're very kind."

"You said earlier that you hadn't wanted to go to them."

"I guess I shouldn't have said that. It's just that—well, Richard has always been my favourite brother, though I love them all, of course. Perhaps it's because I've always had to stick up for him!"

He raised his eyebrows. "Your brother Richard struck me as being well able to stick up for himself."

"Oh, he is, of course. I meant when he's not there. The others don't approve of him, especially Caroline and Janet, Toby's wife."

"And couldn't you have stayed with Richard?"

She shook her head decidedly. "No, it just wasn't on. For one thing he has a tiny flat and then Gillian, the girl he's living with, well, she's very sweet, but you could hardly expect her to welcome the thought of a sister as a permanent addition to the household!"

"Is she permanent herself?" asked Lewis with some amusement.

141

"I wouldn't bet on it. Richard's rather fickle. You should hear Caroline on the subject!"

"I can imagine!" he said treacherously, and they both laughed. "Well, we'd better be pressing on. We've still quite a lot of mileage to cover."

As he switched on the ignition, he leant over on impulse and kissed her lightly on the mouth. Her lips tasted of salt from the winds of Eastbourne. Neither of them made any attempt to prolong the kiss, but Lewis found it inexpressibly sweet. She settled back in her seat with a contented sigh as they turned out onto the road again. He became aware that she was humming very softly under her breath. The tune knifed into him, but after a moment the spasm passed. After all, it only meant that as Laura relaxed Noel rose to the surface. He felt closer to her than he had done for five years, and the sensation was one of deep, enveloping peace.

Chapter 10

OUTWARDLY, Lewis's relationship with Laura had not really changed, but he was aware, and he thought she was too, that the day in Eastbourne had been a landmark for them, that the deliberately superficial kiss had sealed the bond between them.

However, there were also times when he bitterly regretted letting Caroline go while their attraction for each other was still at its height, and perhaps unfairly, he blamed Laura for this. During the hours he was away from her, he was constantly racked with recurring doubts about the whole affair and when he looked back on their conversation at lunch that day, it seemed completely preposterous. He was at a loss to understand how he had even for a moment accepted it.

Yet when he was with her, she had only to use some American expression or suddenly look at him sideways under lowered lids in a manner so entirely Noel's and his heart would begin to pound and he'd be floundering again.

During working hours he did not come into contact much with Edward since, although he did submit articles to the *Courier*, he was free-lance and largely his own master. Without the convenience of an office in which to exchange news and views, he had fallen into the habit of dropping in to the Three Bells most evenings, where journalists from several of the local papers generally met over a drink.

One evening towards the end of June he was later than

usual coming away from Four Winds and arrived at the pub just as a crowd of his friends were leaving.

He glanced at his watch. "Anyone still inside?"

"Yes, Steve said he'd hang on in case you showed up. The advantages of bachelorhood!"

Lewis nodded and pushed his way inside. The little room was crowded as usual, but Steve Barton was the only member of his crowd still there. Lewis joined him at the far end of the curved bar where Caroline had found him that time with Harry. He accepted the beer Steve put on the bar top in front of him, but his mind was still reeling from the combined impact of Laura and Noel.

"Lewis?"

He looked up. "Sorry, did you say something?"

Steve looked at him worriedly, his face creased with concern. "What is it, old lad? Something's obviously on your mind these days. Anything I can do?"

It was exactly the right psychological moment for such an offer, and Lewis succumbed. The relief of being able to talk the whole thing over with a sympathetic but disinterested outsider would, he felt, be boundless.

"You could listen, if you wouldn't mind," he said slowly.

"Glad to. Fire away."

"The devil of it is, I don't know where to start." He looked up, straightened his shoulders and met Steve's eye squarely. "What would you say if I told you I thought the spirit of someone I once knew, and loved, was trying to get in contact with me?"

He waited, more tense than he realized, for Steve's reaction. If it were one of outright scepticism, he would laugh it all off and change the subject, but to his untold relief Steve replied quietly, "I should be extremely interested.

144

Has she succeeded?"

Lewis said abruptly, "You don't think I'm going out of my mind?"

"Not at all. As a matter of fact it's a pet subject of mine. I did a lot of research on it once for some articles that had been commissioned, the whole caboodle, ouija boards, mediums (or is it media?), even poltergeists. And the more I studied it, admittedly in the first instance with my tongue in my cheek, the more I became convinced that there's something in it. That was several years ago, and lately of course there's been a whole spate of magazine articles and television programs on the occult. People are beginning to realize that what they had written off as a lot of cranky make-believe ought to be taken seriously."

Lewis let out his breath in a long sigh. "I can't tell you what a relief it is to hear you say that. I must admit I've always been among the scoffers myself. That's why it's all the harder now to understand what's happening."

"And what is?"

He hesitated. "This won't go any further?"

"My lips are sealed!"

"Well, I think I told you that I used to live in this district. I'd rather not be too specific about either people or places, if you don't mind, but I was always extremely fond of my home, and still am, though the interior at least is now changed almost beyond recognition."

He was silent for a while, trying to think how best to say what he wanted to without actually implicating either Laura or Noel. He hitched himself up onto a stool and leant back against the panelled wall at the end of the bar.

"I don't know whether you know, but I was in the States covering the primaries before the 'sixty-eight Presidential election. I'd met quite a few members of the American press out in Saigon and had a ready-made set of contacts, which of course was invaluable. One of them was the son-in-law of the editor of one of the big New York dailies, which opened up social connections too, and as is usually the case, you tend to find you come up against the same crowd at all the different do's."

"And this is where you met the girl?"

"Yes. Actually she wasn't exactly a girl. She must have been about thirty then. She'd been married for ten years to a man twenty-five years older than herself."

"Ah-hah!"

Lewis said quickly, "No, it wasn't like that. She idolized him. He'd been a friend of the family ever since her childhood. His first wife had run off and left him, apparently, soon after they were married. Anyway, he took—I'll call her 'N'—to her first dances rather in the role of an uncle, introduced her to young people her own age, and so on, but apparently even then she'd decided he was the one she wanted." He emptied his glass and Steve beckoned the barman for a refill.

"Well, when she was sixteen her parents were both killed in a plane crash. She was an only child and she didn't seem to have any relations. Naturally enough she just turned to—him."

"He hasn't got a name either?" Steve enquired with a smile.

"If you don't mind, no."

"Fair enough, carry on. I presume she told you all this herself?"

"Yes. Well, I suppose from then on their marriage was inevitable. He admitted that he'd always loved her, but he was very fair about it and most reluctant to tie her down so young. She was quite frank about being the one who insisted. However, as he was in the regular army and away a lot on active service, it was arranged that she should live with his married sister for a while, and I gather it was tacitly agreed that if she met anyone else, she would be quite free to break things off."

"He certainly seems to have bent over backwards not to take advantage of her."

"Precisely. But as I said, she'd always hero-worshipped him and she wasn't interested in meeting anyone else, so eventually they were married, just before her twentieth birthday."

"When he would have been forty-five."

"Yes. He applied for a home posting and for some years she moved round the country with him and apparently they were very happy. Then the Vietnam War blew up and he was sent out there. By this time, incidentally, she had grown into a very beautiful woman, tall and fair, with an air of quiet dignity about her, and I might add there was no shortage of men who were interested in her. I heard about her long before I met her, the beautiful and remote Mrs. X."

He glanced across at Steve. "Sorry if I'm being somewhat long-winded."

"There's no hurry. A question of filling in the background, I presume?"

"Yes, I think it's relevant. Anyway, she had the reputation of being cool and reserved and not letting anyone within a mile of her."

"Except you?"

Lewis stared down into his glass. "God knows why I should have been singled out to get through to her. The timing might have been to my advantage. Her husband had been away for over four years by then, and I suppose to some extent they were bound to have grown apart. For my part, of course, I fell for her hook, line and sinker. I'd been forewarned, everyone had. Her unapproachability was one of the main attractions in the first instance." He paused, uncomfortably aware of having said much the same thing about Caroline.

"But in your case she reciprocated."

"Not at first. God, she was like a block of ice. I was 'Mr. Castleton' for long enough, and amid all that trans-Atlantic informality that was quite a hurdle. I sometimes think it was partly the fact of my being English that made her notice me. She was a true Anglophile. Apparently several generations back her family had come from Worcestershire. Anyway, she couldn't hear enough about England, and especially my home. I don't know why, but it seemed to fascinate her. Time and again I had to describe it to her—'from the minute you turn in the gateway,' she used to say."

He was silent for so long that Steve prompted gently, "So—what happened next?"

Lewis moved suddenly. "We fell in love and, tragically, she died."

"How?"

"Does it matter?" His voice was brusque. "I'm sorry, I can't talk about that part. Afterwards I went completely to pieces. Everyone put it down to overwork. Incredibly enough we'd managed to keep the whole thing secret. As soon as I could stand on my feet again, I went careering back to Vietnam. I think I almost hoped I'd get blown up myself."

"Did you ever meet her husband?"

"Yes, I did once." He paused. "He was a very forceful man, well over six feet tall with thick, iron-grey hair."

148

"And he never knew about you and his wife?"

"No. That, at least, I could be thankful for."

"And now you think she's trying to get in touch with you."

"Sometimes I do. Sometimes I'm convinced it's all imagination."

"Suppose you tell me?"

"I'd still rather keep off names, Steve. You might gather whom I'm talking about, but even so—"

"Okay, if it makes you feel easier."

"Well, I moved round the world, deliberately seeking out the most dangerous places I could find. My guardian angel, if it exists, must have had its work cut out! I drank too much, I gambled, all the recognized devices for trying to forget something which is unforgettable. Of course none of it worked. Then, in the spring of last year, I suddenly realized the cycle had come round again and they were about to embark on another round of the ballyhoo which would lead up to a Presidential election. And I knew damn well I just couldn't face it. Quite suddenly I longed to be home, here down in Brocklehurst. So I dropped everything and came. I moved into digs in Ledbrook, submitted a few articles to the *Courier* and, to my own amazement, showed every sign of settling down. And I felt more at peace than I had for years."

"Did you go back to the house?"

"My family had sold it years ago. I drove past time and again, but you can't see a great deal from the road. There was an 'Under Offer' notice by the gate, and shortly after it changed to 'Sold,' and then for months there were workmen's vans in the driveway. I wondered what the hell they were doing to the old place."

"And were you aware of—her—at this stage?"

"No, that's quite recent. I happened to meet the new owners of—my old home."

"Still no names!" Steve murmured.

"And as I hoped, when they learnt I had once lived there, they were kind enough to invite me to dinner. There was a girl staying with them—"

"Yes?"

"Apparently she'd talked of seeing some twisted trees at the bottom of the garden. They were no longer there, but they had been when I was a boy."

Steve was leaning towards him now, his eyes intent.

"That was the first thing. Coincidence—all the usual slick explanations. But the night I went to dinner, this girl insisted she'd seen a boy upstairs who told her he'd just been in to see his dead grandmother."

"Ye gods!"

"Firstly, of course, there had been no child in the house at the time. And secondly, almost exactly thirty years before, *I* had been in to see *my* dead grandmother."

Steve gave a low whistle.

"Soon after this, the girl begged to be allowed to write a book about my life, for heaven's sake. And gradually, God knows how, I began to feel she was strangely like—'N.' She 'knew' things I hadn't told her, about my childhood particularly: a clock we once had, a German pilot who came down just outside Ledbrook during the war. It didn't strike me at first, but gradually I came to realize that although I hadn't told *her* about these things, everything that she 'remembered' I *had* told 'N.' "

"Fascinating!"

"That's more or less all. This girl has started to use American expressions which she never did before, she hums 'N's' favourite tune—things like that."

150

"And does she seem aware of what's happening?"

"Up to a point. I don't think she realizes the full significance of it, though. She talks quite openly about the other girl by name, says she was an unhappy presence in the house but is happier now she's being helped."

"My God!"

"Look, Steve, what do you think, honestly?"

"I should get her to a medium if I were you. I could put you in touch with one if you like."

"Thanks, I'll bear it in mind. And thanks for listening. I don't know if it's any clearer in my own mind, but it helped to talk to someone about it."

"I do feel you should take some kind of step to find out exactly what's happening. It's only fair, to both of them."

"You're right, of course."

"There's nothing else you can think of?"

"I don't think so. Oh—this girl did say she dreamt about me before we met and I called her 'N.' "

"So now we have to add precognition to the other complexities!"

"It would seem so."

"Is it only at the house that you're aware of the spirit of the dead girl?"

"No. It used to be, but the influence appears to be gaining ground. She seems able to go now wherever the other girl goes."

Steve's head jerked up. "Possession? God, Lewis, you'll have to watch it. That's something else again. I think the vicar would be your best bet."

"Oh, nonsense! At least not until I find out what it is she wants."

"But don't you see. You might be risking this girl's sanity!"

"Don't worry, I'll keep it in check. And remember you're bound by the silence of the confessional or what-ever."

Steve smiled grimly. "Shows which way your mind's working—I presume you mean a 'D' notice? Anyway, having given my word, I'll keep it, but I can't advise you too strongly to be careful how you handle this. It goes without saying that I'll be on tenterhooks to hear what happens next. If you run into any problems, I'll be pleased to offer what help I can."

"Thanks, Steve."

"I'd better be getting along. You've certainly given me something to think about! Good night, Lewis."

"Good night."

He leant his head back against the wall panelling and watched Steve thread his way round the bar and out of the door. Had it been wise to say so much? Steve would not have much trouble tracking down at least Laura and Four Winds if he put his mind to it, but he was a trustworthy man and Lewis felt he could depend on his silence.

The barman tapped him on the arm. "Sorry, Mr. Castleton, sir, but will you drink up? It's closing time."

"Of course."

He realized everyone was moving slowly towards the door, finished his drink and went with them. High over the fields the moon swung like a golden ball and the warm night air was alive with expectancy. It seemed a sacrilege to drive meekly home, but there was no more exciting alternative. Also, his talk with Steve following on the emotional two hours he had spent with Laura had drained him. Wearily he climbed into his car.

Lights were at the upstairs windows of Four Winds as he passed, but Brocklehurst itself was deserted. The street lamps were strung along the roadway like miniature moons, but their light fell on empty streets and dark, huddled houses. He smiled to himself, understanding and acknowledging Harry's incredulity at his being prepared to spend his life in this backwater. But Harry didn't appreciate that Noel had summoned him back to the one place on earth where she felt able to reach him, and that time and place were immaterial if they could be together again.

With a feeling of acquiescence he turned into the dark, rutted lane that led to the cottage.

Chapter 11

H E D I D N ' T see Laura that weekend. Her youngest brother had come up from Sussex with his wife and baby, prepared apparently to stay for several days. Lewis wondered with grim amusement whether he would be called upon to present himself for inspection as he had when Richard came, but no invitation materialized and on the Monday afternoon Laura phoned.

"Lewis, it's just not worth your coming while Toby and Janet are here. The baby cries all the time and I can't concentrate on anything."

"You sound a little harassed, my dear. Would it help to get away from them for a while? We could always have our discussion here, if Big Brother would allow you to come."

"That's an idea. I am a bit upset. Actually I've rather a headache today, my first for some time. I didn't sleep well and when I finally managed to drop off, I had the most horrible dream." Her voice shook slightly.

"Never mind. Come as soon as you like; I'm in the rest of the day. If you can face pork pie and pickles, I can even offer you supper—but it might make you dream again!"

He gave the cottage a cursory flick with a duster and carried deck-chairs and a rug out into the overgrown garden at the back. Enclosed as it was on all sides, the little garden made a perfect suntrap and the long grass was bleached to hay.

Laura arrived at five o'clock, carrying her tape recorder

and notebooks. "Edward dropped me at the end of the lane." She flopped into a deck-chair and closed her eyes. "What a relief to get away! I adore Toby but he's so terribly analytical! Everything anyone says has to be taken apart, examined and given cross-references. And Janet's as bad. She was a schoolteacher right up until the baby became too obvious. She'll probably farm it out as soon as she can and go back to teaching."

"What an intellectual family you are!" Lewis observed, handing her a glass of ice-cold shandy.

"I know. It's a bit of a drag at times. Toby writes poetry, you know, and he's also art critic to some frightfully erudite magazine or other. And Janet's hobby is pottery— too arty for words! She's always so *intent* on everything. No wonder she gives me a headache! She's only a year older than I am, but she treats me like a backward six-year-old. Heaven help that baby if she doesn't turn out to be a genius!"

"Funny how different your brothers' tastes in women are," Lewis said, smiling. "Is Janet way out like Gillian, or stately and beautiful like Caroline?"

"Neither. She has long dark hair and very straight brows and she wears glasses and flat shoes. You know," she added unexpectedly, "I thought at one time you rather fancied Caroline."

Lewis said carefully, "Doesn't everyone? She's a most attractive woman."

"I was very upset about it. Of course, I thought it was on Edward's behalf, but I guess it must have been Noel's."

"In any case, you wouldn't have approved?"

"No," she answered quietly, "I just couldn't have borne it. I'm glad it all fizzled out."

He didn't reply for a moment, then he said diffidently,

"And what are we going to talk about today?"

"I don't know. To tell you the truth I feel lazy, not like working at all."

"Probably due to your disturbed night." He paused. "Are you going to tell me about your midsummer night's dream?"

"Oh, it was, wasn't it? I didn't realize. It was nothing to do with fairies, though." She shivered and changed the subject quickly. "By the way, I bumped into Paul Denver yesterday. He wants me to stop seeing you!"

"Oh! Might I ask why?"

"He doesn't think you're good for me."

"Wise man! I've never been good for any woman!"

"Even Noel?"

"Especially Noel, bless her heart. And do you intend to take any notice of Denver's warning?"

"I can't, can I?"

His eyes moved over her small face tilted to the sun, the delicate bone structure, the curve of her throat. She looked so defenceless and vulnerable, and Noel was so strong—stronger than he himself had ever been.

"No, my dear, I don't suppose you can." Incredibly he felt a small stirring of jealousy. "Is he in love with you?"

Her eyes flew open. "Paul? Good heavens, no! He bites my head off every time I see him these days!"

"Even so, I think it's likely that he is. He seems to seek you out a good deal and to have your welfare very much at heart." Lewis could find it in his own heart to pity him.

"I think that's because at first, when I was frightened of you, I told him about it."

"No wonder he regards me as a sinister influence!"

They were silent for a while and the sun slowly moved across the colourless grass. Lewis wondered if she were asleep, but he was perfectly content to relax in the warmth, knowing she was there and occasionally searching her face for hidden signs of Noel.

At about six-thirty he brought out the pork pie and a large crusty loaf which he cut into thick slices. There was a strong cheese, pickles and a dish of spring onions, and they ate hungrily. Afterwards, Laura insisted on carrying the dirty dishes into the kitchen and washing them.

"Hardly on a par with the kitchen at Four Winds, is it?" Lewis said ruefully, watching her wipe down the ancient wooden draining board.

"Hardly, but I feel more at home here."

"Do you, Laura?" For a moment he wanted above everything to take her in his arms and kiss her, but already she had moved away and the chance was gone. Slowly he followed her outside again. The sun was off the garden now but its heat still lingered. Laura was standing on the path surveying the weeds and brambles which ran riot.

"You know, you can hire machinery to cut away all this," she remarked.

"It's not worth it. No one ever sees it and anyway it would only come back again. I'm afraid I haven't the perseverance to be a gardener."

"Is that a gate in the far wall? I hadn't noticed it before."

"Yes, it leads into the wood. Lord knows why. Perhaps the old dears who used to live here went foraging for firewood."

"Have you ever used it?"

"No, I'm not given to walking in woods. Not alone, anyway!"

"Can we go now and see where it leads? I could do with a bit of exercise."

"If you like. The trickiest part will be getting out of the garden!"

Carefully they manoeuvered the treacherous wild rose thorns and clinging strands of the creepers which matted the undergrowth, and with only a few scrapes and scratches they managed to reach the gate. It was tied together with a fraying piece of rope, hanging drunkenly on broken hinges. Beyond it, the cool dim reaches of Gillet's Wood stretched silently away.

Lewis held the gate up while Laura went through. There was a dusty, barky smell and dried twigs snapped under their feet, startling birds which were pecking in the undergrowth so that they flew upwards with a clattering of wings.

"I wonder how long it is since anyone came along here?" Laura said softly.

"Lord knows, but I doubt if there's any need to whisper!"

"It's almost like being in church." She peered upwards into the green cloistered arches of the branches which met overhead. "Do you think we should leave a trail of pebbles to guide us back, like Hansel and Gretel?"

He smiled and took her hand and they walked on some way until they came to a small clearing. Probably his surmise about the firewood had been correct, because an ancient pile of crumbling logs was piled in the centre, overgrown now by moss and wild bluebells. Laura gave a little shiver.

"It's rather eerie, isn't it? I wonder if when they, whoever they were, left this place for the last time, they realized it *was* the last time, or if they were confidently expecting to come back for the rest of the logs the next day."

"That's quite a thought."

158

"Perhaps it's as well that so many 'last times' come and go without our recognizing them for what they are."

"Perhaps."

"Or would the very fact of knowing somehow enable you to take avoiding action and thereby cancel the necessity for its being the last time after all? Paul and I had a conversation along those lines once."

"Precognition?"

"Yes. For instance, when Mother and I set out on that fatal journey, suppose some inner voice had said, 'This is the last journey she'll ever make.' Obviously we'd never have set out, and perhaps—" She turned her head away from him and he gripped her hand comfortingly.

"Don't grieve any more, Laura. She couldn't have known anything."

After a moment, still with her head averted, she answered shakily, "How do we know? She *must* have known, just for a split second, that she was going to die."

"Stop it!" His voice rang out and she turned and looked at him, her face luminous in the diffused green light.

"I think perhaps I'd better tell you what I dreamt last night after all."

Something in her tone jerked his heart into sudden rapid beating. Every instinct warned him to stop her, to insist that he didn't want to hear about it after all, but she was already speaking again in that slow, far-away voice and all he could do was stand helplessly and listen.

"I seemed to be in a car," she was saying, "and I thought at first it was going to be one of those terrible dreams where I relived the accident. It happened every night in the hospital. Then I realized that this time was different. For one thing, the car had a left-hand drive."

If she felt the violent tremor which shook him, she gave

159

no sign other than to tighten her grip on his hand.

"I was in the driving seat, but the steering wheel seemed to be miles away from me and was receding all the time and my hands were wobbly and uncontrollable, like cotton-wool."

He said in a strangled voice, "Laura—please—"

"There was a newspaper stand on the sidewalk. The headlines on the papers were something about Kennedy— 'Kennedy flies to Frisco' or something like that. I tried to say something to you, but I couldn't seem to turn my head."

"To—me?" He brought the words out with difficulty.

Her eyes refocussed momentarily. "That's strange. I didn't see who was sitting beside me, but I knew it was you. The car seemed to be going faster and faster and I'd no control over it at all. Suddenly we came to a corner, and my useless hands couldn't turn the wheel. There was a terrific, jarring crash—I think the nearside door flew open—and almost immediately an explosion which seemed to be in my own head." After a second's pause she added flatly, "I knew that it had killed me."

She stopped speaking and the only sound in the suddenly silent wood was his harsh, grating breath. He said through shaking lips, "God in heaven! Oh, God, God!"

She stirred a little against him, and when she spoke again it was in a voice that bore no resemblance to her own. "You put something in the drinks, didn't you, Lew?"

He stared at her, his face livid, and then with a low moan pulled her into his arms. "Darling, I never meant you to go alone—you did understand that, didn't you? I've never forgiven myself for coming out of it alive. Noel, forgive me!" His mouth fastened on hers and exultantly he felt her automatic response as her arms came round his neck. Then, as he continued to hold and kiss her, they faltered, withdrew, and at last pushed frantically against his chest. She tore herself free and, with ice-cold sweat pouring down his face, he opened his eyes to stare with a kind of numb horror into Laura's frightened face. Laura? Laura!

"Lewis—stop it—I'm not—"

Somehow the tumult inside him abated slightly, but even when he could finally speak, he had no control over the actual words. He heard himself say, "What in God's name do you want of me?"

But it was Laura who answered tremulously, "Lewis, make her stop now. Please."

He shook his head and pulled her gently back into his arms. She stood limp as a rag doll with her pale head against his chest, scarcely seeming to breathe while in contrast his own breath was still as laboured as a pair of ancient bellows.

"Laura—" The name was a token of his reasserted sanity, and he said it again to savour the comfort of it. "Laura, you must see that I can't stand much more of this."

She didn't move, but he felt her intense concentration, as if every fibre of her being awaited his next words. When he didn't go on, she said expressionlessly, "I can't stand it either, but I'm not sure she'll let either of us go now. Don't you want her back after all?"

"How can I answer that? It's a kind of madness. The last five years have been spent forcing myself to realize that I'd lost her. At times I was able to accept it. There were other women, periods of time when I was able to forget for a while."

"In other words it happened as she'd said. The peak of agony did pass with time, but you hadn't given her the chance to prove it. Perhaps that was why she willed you to come back to Brocklehurst."

"God!" he interrupted harshly. "I didn't want the chance myself! Surely you—she—can't doubt that I'd a thousand times rather have gone with her! If it hadn't been for that door flying open so that I was flung clear—"

Laura said wearily, "Take me home, Lewis."

Slowly, with his arm supporting her, they made their way in silence back through the wood and the little rickety gate into the waiting wilderness of the cottage garden. The air was thickening now and it was difficult for their eyes to make out the recorder and notebooks underneath the deck-chair where Laura had dropped them hours before. He stooped to retrieve them and she accepted them with a nod. She seemed drained, depleted.

When a few minutes later he stopped the car in the driveway of Four Winds, the sound of voices reached them from the terrace and Edward called, "That you, Lewis? Have you time for a drink? My younger brother and his wife are here."

Laura said quietly, "You go, but if you don't mind, I think I'll go straight in. I'm exhausted."

"Of course." He had not yet had time to assess his own reactions to the scene in the wood nor its possible consequences and he was still bewildered and confused. A little normal companionship before he had to be alone again would be very welcome.

They went together round the corner of the house to the group on the terrace and Laura made her excuses and went inside. The room behind was in darkness and Caroline emerged from it, a glass in her hand.

162

"If we put the lights on, we're inundated with moths," she explained.

"What can I get you to drink?"

Lewis moved after her into the dimness. "Whisky, please." A waft of her perfume reached him on the warm air and his senses stirred with the memories it brought. Beautiful, normal Caroline. The intermittent regrets he had had about ending their affair returned without warning in a flood which overwhelmed him, coming as it did as a direct and violent reaction against the intricacies and madness of Laura.

His voice shook as he said softly, "How are you, Caroline?"

"Extremely well, thank you." Hers was breathless.

"Are your visitors staying long?" The question was meaningless, simply a way of prolonging their moment alone. He didn't even register her reply. She held out his glass and he took it, feeling her tremble as his fingers brushed against hers. "Caroline—"

She said in a staccato voice, "Did no one ever tell you, Lewis, that you can't have your cake and eat it?"

Edward's voice called, "Can you manage, darling, or shall I come?"

"It's all right, I've done it now."

She brushed past him, her body momentarily framed against the window as she stepped outside. He followed her, the blood thundering in his ears. Her rebuff did not worry him, it was only to be expected. She was still very much aware of him, and the knowledge filled him with excitement.

Out on the terrace he was introduced to Toby and Janet, but it was too dark to make out their features. He sat in the chair Edward had pulled up and lit a cigarette, deliberately filling his mind with evocative thoughts of Caroline to blot out the pulsating implications of Laura's dream.

"I believe you've nobly submitted to baring your soul to my sister?" Toby Hardy remarked idly.

A tremor shook him. His soul—who had charge of it? He heard in a daze Caroline's low laugh. "I trust it hasn't gone that far!"

"But one has to confess all to a biographer, surely?" put in Janet in her clear, rather clipped voice.

"Not that I'm aware of," Lewis returned as steadily as he could. Especially not if she knew everything already.

"Anyway," observed Edward, "the whole point of Laura's deciding on Lewis was to exploit this incomprehensible longing she had to write about violence."

"Yes, did you ever get to the bottom of that? She's always been such a gentle little thing, it struck me as being entirely out of character."

A wail interrupted them from the open window overhead.

"Oh blast, Lucy's alarm has gone for the ten o'clock feed!" Janet stood up and stretched. "What joy it will be when she goes through from six to six!" She nodded vaguely in Lewis's direction. "Nice to have met you, Mr. Castleton, but I'm afraid I must ask you to excuse me. Duty calls."

"Want any help?" Toby offered without enthusiasm.

"It would shake you if I said yes!" his wife retorted over her shoulder.

Lewis let their voices wash over him and felt some of the tenseness begin to dissolve. It was all so normal, so everyday, that anything as blatantly abnormal as the thoughts that had jostled in his head earlier simply could not be countenanced. He must take hold of himself. He might not survive a second nervous collapse. He realized that Edward was speaking to him.

"How long do you think all this will take? We can hardly get a word out of Laura these days! It will be pleasant to be able to hold a normal conversation with her again!"

Normal—that word again. Lewis stirred uneasily. What would happen when the book was finished? Would Noel be reluctant, as Laura had hinted, ever to let them go?

He forced himself to answer Edward. "I'm not really sure. It seems to be going well, I think." But at the mention of Laura, all his latent fears had risen again and it was impossible any longer for him to sit there calmly talking. He drained his glass. "I hope I'll be invited to the literary lunch to launch it!" he said with a forced laugh, getting to his feet. "No, don't get up, but I must be going. Thanks for the drink. Good night."

His words embraced them all, but his eyes rested for a moment on Caroline's shadowed face. If only she had nothing to do with Four Winds, he might be able to anticipate a possible renewal of their relationship without all the attendant misgivings the house always conjured up. Perhaps after all it had been a mistake to return to Brocklehurst. But perhaps, again, the decision to return had not been his in the first place.

Chapter 12

Lᴇᴡɪs did not sleep well that night. During the long dark hours his mind, refusing to be diverted, scuttled backwards and forwards over the sudden dangers this new development had opened up to himself as well as to Laura. Where would it end? After all this time, these five years of penal servitude he had forced himself to survive, for it all suddenly to blow up again—

He leant over the washbasin, peering into the shaving mirror as he scraped the cream off his face, and suddenly his hand jerked, nicking the skin and raising a tiny red bead in the whiteness. Behind him, reflected in the mirror, stood Laura.

"Is it really you or just another of your apparitions?" he asked brutally, bending down to sluice his face under the tap. He reached for his towel and rubbed it vigorously round his face and neck.

"I'm sorry if I frightened you," she said quietly.

"What the hell are you doing here at this time in the morning?"

"It's ten o'clock."

"The devil it is! I must have fallen asleep after all."

"Shall I fix some coffee?"

"It might help."

She moved from the doorway back into the kitchen and he could hear her turning on the tap, the plop of the gas jet and her low, inevitable humming of Noel's tune. The sane, everydayness of the cheap mirror, the soapy stick of shaving cream, wavered and blurred into the shifting miasma of uncertainty and fear. He gripped the edge of the washbasin, head down, wrestling with the doubts and terrors that assailed him. She couldn't know, and yet she did. The crucial point was, did she realize how much she knew?

"Coffee's ready." Was it Noel's voice, or Laura's? He could no longer distinguish between them. Slowly, lumberingly, he made his way through to the sun-filled kitchen. She held out his shirt and he put it on and absently began to button it. She sat down at the table, both hands clasped round the hot mug as though, in the warm airlessness of this June morning, she was cold.

He said with an effort, "You still haven't told me why you've come."

"She asked me to."

"Why?"

"So that you can tell me the whole story."

"She's already told you herself." This conversation—they must both be insane, he thought dazedly.

"Only parts of it. I need to have it all clear."

"Oh, you do?" He leant forward belligerently in his chair.

"Relax, honey."

His face contorted as his hand snaked out, fastening over her wrist. "Noel?" His eyes searched her face with fanatical despair. "What do *you* want me to do?"

Under the laser beam of his concentration Laura's features shifted and blurred into a likeness of the face in the photograph in his desk.

"I want you to stay with me, Lew. Always."

Laura stirred and sighed, gently extracting her hand from his. His face was haggard as he stared at her. "Who are you now?" he asked raggedly.

"You've got to stop her, Lewis, because I can't. I only wanted to help her, but she won't be content with that any longer. She's getting stronger all the time. I haven't any control now to stop her when she wants to take over."

"She was always strong," he said slowly. "Once she made her mind up on something she would go through with it, whatever the cost."

"And whoever got hurt in the process?"

"Yes." He stared down at the table between them.

"And she decided not to leave her husband?"

"But he'd already left her—for four bloody years!"

"That's not quite the same thing."

"Nevertheless, she was weakening. If we'd had another few months, perhaps even weeks, I think I could have talked her round, but time was running out on all sides. As soon as I'd attended the California primary, I was supposed to be flying to Paris. The Vietnam peace talks had started the month before and I wanted to be able to report first hand. It was one of the main issues in the election, of course. I was doing my damnedest to persuade her to come with me. I couldn't face the thought of leaving her with nothing definitely decided, and then, at that crucial moment, old Balfour had to get himself wounded."

"Balfour?" Her voice broke in on his attention like a clarion. She was staring at him wide-eyed as comprehension began to struggle to the surface. *She was General Balfour's wife?*

Too late, he realized what his slip had cost him. Yet surely in time Noel would have told her anyway. He could only watch as she slotted the information into place like the final missing piece of a jigsaw puzzle.

"Of course," she said softly. "His wife was killed in a

168

car accident as he was being flown home. Who was talking about—? It was Mr. Sandilands, at the Howards' party, the day I met you."

He waited, not breathing.

"He said he thought her death wasn't an accident, that there'd been someone else with her—*you*, Lewis!"

His eyes held hers with a sick resignation.

She went on in a whisper, "It must have been the most fantastic shock for you, coming so unexpectedly after all that time."

"Yes," he replied woodenly at last. "It blew up in my face that day without any warning. You, and Sandilands. At the time I didn't realize it was you who was the greater threat."

"You thought of him as a threat? Of course, he said he was going to look into the crash when he got back to the States." There was a silence which stretched between them, taut as an elastic band which eventually must snap. "It was lucky for you he died, wasn't it?"

His eyes didn't leave her face. "I suppose you could say that." He waited, every nerve screaming, for her next comment, but when it came, it was not what he was expecting and he raised his arm to brush away the sweat that was running into his eyes.

"Did you kill her, Lewis?"

When he could speak, he said jaggedly, "I meant to kill us both. I still don't know how I came out of it alive. God knows, I didn't intend to."

"A suicide pact?"

"Not exactly. I hadn't discussed it with her."

"Tell me."

He took an automatic gulp of coffee and almost gagged at the unexpected coldness of it. "You know most of it. As

169

I told you, she was slowly beginning to come round to my way of thinking. Not Paris, perhaps, but I think she might have written to Clark and told him the position. He'd always said he wouldn't stand in her way. It would have been unpleasant, of course, 'Hero's wife deserts him as he fights for democracy'—all that crap, but we could have lived it down. We'd have left the States anyway." He grimaced. "We might have come here and reclaimed Four Winds. That would really have appealed to her. Anyway, I heard on the radio that he'd been wounded and would be flown home as soon as he'd recovered enough to travel. I went straight round to her apartment." He put his hands suddenly over his face. "Don't make me go through that again."

"She said that under the circumstances it was out of the question to leave him; that you should go to Paris as you'd intended and try to forget about her; that in time the worst of the pain would fade."

"Exactly," he agreed. "You might have been there!" His eyes went over her dully. "Perhaps you were."

"What then?"

"Oh, I lost my head. Said she couldn't really have loved me in the first place, all the usual recriminations. It was unfair. I knew how she felt, but I was so appalled at the thought of losing her. She was very white and composed and the more I ranted and raved, the calmer she became. In the end I flung out of the house."

"Yes?"

"Well, I drank myself insensible and went on drinking more or less continuously for two or three days. I did think of doing away with myself, but I knew she'd feel she was to blame. The only solution seemed for both of us to die, together. At the time it seemed quite logical. Then I heard they were flying Balfour home and I had to move quickly. I rang Noel, told her we couldn't part as we had and suggested she should drive out with me to a motel we'd used before for a last evening together. She agreed, of course, and picked me up in her car. I hadn't one in New York. The traffic frightened the daylights out of me."

"And you put something in the drinks?"

"In hers, yes. I'd worked out it would take effect before we got back home."

"Why not in yours too?"

"Because I wanted to be fully conscious of every minute that I had left with her. And because if something went wrong and she passed out earlier, I had to have my wits about me to get her out of the car."

"You didn't mind the thought of being conscious when you actually crashed?"

"No. In a perverted kind of way I was almost looking forward to it—going out with one hell of a bang."

She looked at him with a kind of wonder and then asked, "What did you use? Sleeping pills?"

"Yes, ground down."

"It didn't occur to you that you might have caused a serious accident involving other people?"

"No," he replied with devastating candour, "I didn't think of anyone but ourselves. I can remember every detail of that evening, with her breaking down at last as I seemed to be resigned, pleading with me to say that I understood, that in time we'd be able to think of each other without pain and just be grateful for what we'd had, that we weren't the first people to fall in love and have to part. You know the kind of thing."

"And none of it made you change your mind?"

"No. Quite simply, I didn't believe it. I didn't want to live without her, and I convinced myself that despite what she said, she felt the same. It was just to be a way of putting us both out of our misery."

"When did the powder begin to take effect?"

"Just before we left. She said she felt sleepy. It was very hot in the motel and we went out to the car. I held her for the last time—" His voice shook. "We both knew that, but for different reasons. We stayed there for quite a while, partly because I couldn't bear to let her go and partly to be sure the powder was working. She did say at one stage, 'I don't think I'm fit to drive,' but I told her she was in better shape than I was. In a way it was true. And I think that by that time she didn't really care what happened either. I remember watching the silent tears pouring down her face, and I was glad, *glad* that neither of us had to go on much longer." He was silent for a long time, then he said abruptly, "You know the rest—exactly as you dreamt it."

"You were flung clear?"

"Yes, well clear into some bushes. I was knocked out cold but—can you believe it?—except for a few bruises and scratches I wasn't hurt at all. Physically, that is. Can you begin to imagine how I felt when I realized what had happened? The car burst into flames almost immediately, apparently, when the petrol tank exploded, and someone was on the scene straightaway. They made a cursory examination round about, according to the next day's papers, but they didn't find me in my bushes and so obviously they assumed she'd been alone. By the time I came round, all the hoo-ha had died down, they'd taken her away and towed off what was left of the car. I remember wandering along in the middle of the highway waiting for some vehicle to knock me down, but I must have had the proverbial drunkard's protection, because none did. Eventually a car drew up alongside and the driver said, 'You sure look in need of a lift home, buddy!' I tried to resist him but he hauled me inside and I remember mumbling the name of the hotel where I was staying. So that was that. I seemed unable to get myself killed."

"And no one ever suspected you were involved with her?"

"No one. Her 'untouchable' reputation certainly stood her in good stead. Also, of course, we'd been quite fanatic about only meeting in out-of-the-way places, and she always insisted on wearing dark glasses."

"So what happened?"

"There were headlines in all the papers, poor old Balfour had to be told, one helluva fuss. I was in a state of total shock. A couple of days later Ed Berry, one of my contacts, called for me to join their party flying to California to hear Kennedy. I was like a zombie, I just did what I was told, so I went with them. But immediately after the shooting, I simply went under. I was in hospital in Los Angeles for weeks, getting psychiatric treatment, shock therapy, the lot. They told me afterwards they didn't think I'd make it. For myself, I'd rather not have done."

"And the truth of Noel's death never came out."

"No. On that flight to Los Angeles I heard Ed and the others talking about it. There'd been one or two reports in the press that other motorists had thought there were two people in the car, and also that she'd been driving erratically before the accident, but the fire ruled out any possibility of testing for alcohol or anything, so they never discovered the presence of the sleeping pills. God only knows what raised old Sandilands' suspicions." His eyes went intently to her face. "Did he say any more about it, that night you had dinner with him?"

"A little, I think, more or less what you've just said yourself, about people reporting there was someone else in the car. He'd deduced it could have been a lover, but surely he wouldn't have been able to prove anything after so long?"

"I don't know."

He watched the change come over her, almost uncaring. Her hands flattened on the table as she levered herself slowly to her feet, while her face seemed to cave in on itself, making nose and chin unnaturally prominent.

"But," she whispered at last, "you couldn't afford to take the chance. Could you?"

"As you say."

"You killed him! That nice, pleasant little man—"

"Laura, I'd no choice. If he started ferreting around, the man who took me home that night might suddenly remember finding someone wandering in a dazed condition in that area. And if he also remembered which hotel he took me to, the rest would be easy. God, haven't I paid enough already? What further punishment do I deserve?"

"So you killed him," she repeated. She seemed unable to take it in. She seemed far more shocked by this revelation than by his admittance of causing Noel's death. Possibly the personal element came into it.

"I'd intended to do it the previous evening, in case he said anything more to you. Not that you'd have had any reason to connect it with me, of course. However, I didn't get the opportunity then so it had to be the Tuesday. I saw you all drive away—"

"And it was all for nothing, anyway. Fenella will probably dig it out now, if it's possible to dig anything."

174

"His assistant? Yes, I didn't realize how closely she was involved until that evening I had dinner at Four Winds and then, since she was flying back to the States the next day, it was too late to do anything about it."

"Thank God!" Her voice cracked.

His chair jarred on the floor. "Don't look at me like that! Noel, are you there? You see, don't you, that it was for your sake too?"

Laura said through paper-white lips, "You're mad!"

He came swiftly round the table and seized her arms. "Noel! Do you understand?"

She struggled frantically to free her body from his vise-like grip and her mind from the cloudy advent of Noel. "Let me go! Lewis, let me go!" And then, as body and mind both succumbed to greater forces, she relaxed in his arms and he heard her say, "It's all right, baby. Of course I understand."

"Noel—she might tell someone—"

"No, sweetheart, I won't let her. It's all right." She was holding him now, soothing and calm, and gradually his tumultuous breathing quietened. At last Laura moved away from him.

"Noel?"

"It's Laura, Lewis. I must go. Edward has to attend a dinner in Sussex tonight, so Toby and Janet are going back with him and he'll spend the night at their house. I promised I'd be back in time to say good-bye."

Her manner was as calm and normal as if the preceding hour had been wiped from her mind. How much did she remember?

"You look all in," she said gently. "Go back to bed and try to rest."

He ran a hand wearily through his hair. "I might. What

about this evening? Since your brother and his family will have gone—"

"I suppose it will be all right. Caroline's playing bridge this afternoon, but she'll be back about six. Come and have dinner with us like you did before."

He looked at her blankly, remembering from a great distance last night's renewed desire for Caroline. Had it really only been last night? How they entangled him, the three of them—Caroline exciting his body, Noel clinging to his mind, Laura seemingly in possession of both mind and body. Which of them would claim him in the end?

She had taken hold of his arm with an anxious frown. "Lewis—are you all right? Will you come for dinner this evening?"

"Yes," he mumbled, "I'll come." After she had gone, he barely remembered stumbling upstairs and falling across the bed. It was more like a drugged coma than normal sleep, and it lasted until well into the afternoon. He awoke to find the full force of the sun pouring down on him and his shirt plastered against his chest.

He sat up slowly and looked at his watch. Half-past three. He must have slept for over four hours. He went back downstairs, stopping short as he saw his own and Laura's mugs still on the table, half full of cold coffee. God, he'd hoped that was all some weird kind of dream. Had it been to Laura he had confessed Sandilands' murder, or to Noel? Surely it was Laura who had stood staring at him with such horror. But Noel had promised to see to it and certainly Laura's attitude when she left him had been devoid of any hint of accusation. All he could do was trust to Noel and hope for the best.

As it happened, Caroline was approaching Four Winds from the direction of Ledbrook as he turned into the gateway himself. He got out of the car and went over to her as she drew to a halt in the driveway. She had a wide white band across her gold hair and her smooth brown arms jingled with gold bracelets. After weeks of attention riveted on Laura's pale, colourless little form, Caroline was vividly beautiful and his colour-starved eyes feasted on her in sensuous delight.

"If you keep staring at me like that, you'll make me blush!" she commented, looking up at him with, he felt, deliberate provocation.

"I was just thinking you look good enough to eat!"

"I think crab salad would be more nourishing. That's all you'll be offered, anyway!"

"And for dessert?" He opened the door of the car and helped her out. Her bare arm was silky-smooth under his fingers. For an instant her deep blue eyes stared tantalizingly back at him. His hand tightened, drew her fractionally towards him.

"Strawberries and cream!" she replied, and laughed.

His breathing quickened. "No choice?"

"Positively none. You made your choice some time ago."

"Caroline, I was out of my mind! You can't—"

"Sh!" She glanced over his shoulder and he felt her stiffen. Turning, he saw that Laura was standing watching them from the doorway.

PART 4

Noel

Chapter 13

ALL THROUGH dinner she watched them playing their little game, Caroline careless and provocative, Lewis intent on her every word and movement, and the hurt bewildered anger spread through her like a creeping fire. After all this, after all these years of searching, when they had finally come together again, this woman had only to toss her lovely head and glance at him invitingly under her long eyelids for him to give up all pretence and devote his entire attention to her. They were lovers, she was sure of it now, and the throbbing shafts of jealousy thrust down inside her until she almost cried out.

Caroline said, "Laura, you're not eating a thing. Aren't you hungry?"

She looked back at her with choking hatred and resentment. "No." Why, why had she agreed to Lewis coming here this evening, when Edward was away?

"Don't you feel well?"

The words triggered off a warning inside her head. The next step would be to suggest she went to lie down, leaving them alone.

"I'm all right," she said sullenly.

Lewis smiled at her with absent-minded kindness. "It's probably the heat. It is very oppressive."

The leaden weight settled somewhere in her stomach. It was understandable, of course. Much as he still loved her, he could not completely accept the manifestations of her presence, and she knew despairingly that the more she made that presence felt, the more she was in danger of driving him into Caroline's arms. A spirit without a body was not enough after all. If Laura were as attractive as Caroline, she might have more chance of sustaining his interest, for Lewis had always been susceptible to a woman's beauty. But it was Laura's very insignificance that had made the take-over so easy; Caroline was stronger in every way.

She pushed her chair back. "Let's go in the garden, Lewis. At least there might be a bit of a breeze there."

He hesitated, his eyes still on Caroline. "Do you feel up to working?"

"Of course."

Caroline said carelessly, "Off you go then, and Mrs. Baines can clear the table. Don't worry about me. I have some letters to write." She turned dismissively away to replace the stopper in the wine decanter.

They went together out through the open French windows and across to the pear tree.

"Lewis!" There was frustrated despair in the cry and he turned to her in surprise. "What do I have to do to make you notice me? This?" She caught hold of his face between her hands and dragged it down to her lips. For a moment he was stiff and unyielding, then, as she asserted herself, his arms came tightly round her. This, then, was the answer—a body of her own for him to hold again.

After a while, Laura opened heavy eyelids to find him scanning her face.

"When we were talking this morning—" he began anxiously.

"About Mr. Sandilands?"

"So you do remember. I shouldn't have told you, I realize that now. It's too much of a burden. You might feel—"

She laid a finger on his lips. "I promised, didn't I?"

His mouth twisted. "One of you did!"

"For both of us. It's finished, Lewis. Telling anyone wouldn't bring him back."

"Hardly the reaction of a responsible member of society, my love!"

"But I'm not, am I? Responsible, I mean. Not for anyone, even myself." She moved away from him and sat down in one of the deck-chairs. After a moment he did the same.

He said quietly, "Do you really think you can accept it, Laura? I dare say I could count on a certain amount of loyalty from Noel, but I've no right to expect it from you."

She gave a little shiver. "I gather Noel has every intention of imposing her own set of values on me too, whether I like it or not. Lewis, I can't keep control any more. Several times lately she's been too strong for me."

He looked at her curiously. "Have you any warning when she's coming?"

"Very little; it all happens so quickly. There's a strange, tingling sensation that seems to run right through my body, and almost as soon as I'm aware of it, she's there."

"Do you think Edward has noticed anything?"

"I doubt it. She always lets me keep the upper hand when he's there." She hesitated, flashing him a look under her lashes. "I'm not so sure about Caroline, though."

He looked away from her. "As a matter of fact I think I said something to Caroline at one time, before I realized quite what was happening."

183

"Have you ever discussed it with anyone else?"

"I did mention it pretty generally to a chap I know who's interested in ESP. No names, of course, but even so, I've regretted it since. The fewer people who know about it, the better. Didn't you say you mentioned something about it to Paul Denver?"

"Yes."

"Have you seen him lately?"

"I saw him on Sunday, as I told you, when he asked me to keep away from you. Actually, he was trying to make me agree to see a psychiatrist."

He stiffened. "You didn't, did you?"

"No, but even if I did, there's little he could do. After all, I'm perfectly rational in myself and so is she. There's nothing wrong with either of our minds separately, it's just the merging which is so frightening. Lewis—"

"Yes?"

She flushed. "I don't know how to say this, but—please keep away from Caroline."

He stared at her, nonplussed. "For Edward's sake, or Noel's?"

"Both, but mainly for her own. I honestly think Noel might—try to harm her in some way."

"Surely that wouldn't be possible?"

"It would if she used me."

Annoyance and disbelief struggled for expression on his face. "Are you really trying to tell me—?"

"Yes, I am. All through dinner she was getting more and more upset. She—I—desperately wanted to hurt Caroline, to lash out, remove her somehow."

After a moment he said stiffly, "Well, if it's any consolation to either of you, Caroline was not open to my advances, such as they were."

"That wasn't the impression that came over."

"Nevertheless I assure you it's true."

"Thank God."

"Yes. Well, that might be your reaction."

She smiled faintly. "Poor Lewis, you do have trouble with your women!"

"It was still Noel when we first came out here, wasn't it?"

"Who kissed you? Of course."

"Do you mind her using you like that?"

"No, because by that time she was thinking for me, so I felt as she did."

"And now? Suppose I were to kiss you now?"

She said slowly, "*I'm* not in love with you, if that's what you're asking."

He leant forward, staring down at the grass between his feet. "Has it ever occurred to you—?"

"That she wants you to marry me?"

He was watching her without moving. "Yes. I wasn't sure if you realized that."

"Surely it wouldn't be possible anyway? I mean, her husband's still alive."

"But she isn't! Lord, what a mess!"

"If I married you, Lewis, it would be the end of me." She smiled at the expression on his face. "I mean just that. She would take over completely. I—couldn't."

He said quietly, "We'll give it time. You might change your mind."

"You mean *she* might change it." She looked across at him curiously. "Do *you* want to marry me?"

"I don't know, Laura. As you say, it would really be Noel—"

"So you do. I sometimes feel I no longer have any

choice, that between you, you and Noel—"

"Hush, sweetheart." He covered her fluttering hands with his own, and immediately they quietened. "Don't you personally feel anything for me at all?"

"I don't know what I feel any more. Yes, I suppose in a way I do. I certainly feel more complete when you're there, even when Noel isn't dominant, though I guess it's still due to her influence." She gave a little half-laugh and glanced at him shyly. "To be honest, I rather think I was a little bit jealous of Caroline myself at dinner!"

His hand tightened on hers. "You needn't be. I can't deny that I find her extremely attractive, but it's a purely physical thing. I never pretended otherwise."

"Whereas with Noel it's purely emotional?"

"Not when she's using you."

She digested that in silence. He persisted, "And your response wasn't wholly emotional either, was it?"

"It was her response."

"But your body."

Her hands clenched. "It's as I thought, then. She won't be content with taking over my mind, she needs my body too. Permanently."

He said sharply, "Laura—don't!"

She didn't seem to hear him. "She's probably realized it already. I shall have to be on my guard the whole time—even when I'm asleep, if that's possible." She turned back to him, eyes dilated in her frightened face. "Hold me, Lewis! Please hold me!"

He dropped onto the grass beside her and gathered her into his arms and after a few minutes she relaxed a little. He kissed her gently and though she trembled, she made no other response. Noel had not returned. He stood up, drawing her to her feet.

186

"It's time I went. You're exhausted and so am I. Come with me while I say good-bye to Caroline—and you can tell Noel she has nothing to fear there."

Caroline was sitting at the desk in the sitting-room, the light from the lamp above her burnishing her hair to strands of gold. She looked up and something in her eyes told Laura that she had witnessed their embrace.

"Thank you for the meal, Caroline. It was excellent, as always. Laura and I are both in need of an early night, so I'm going now. Give my regards to Edward."

Caroline said levelly, "I see you had a choice of dessert after all."

Laura glanced from one to the other, sensing the under-current between them without quite understanding it.

"As you say."

"I must confess, Lewis, that I'm full of admiration for your adaptability!" There was a brittle note in her voice which jarred on Laura's ears, making her wonder if Lewis had been less than truthful in his assessment of the situation between them. She felt his arm tense about her shoulders before he dropped it abruptly, and his face had flushed a dark red.

"Perhaps you'll excuse me? Don't see me to the door. I'll walk back along the terrace. Sleep well, Laura."

He nodded briefly in Caroline's direction and was gone. The sound of his footsteps reached them clearly, and the slam of the car door. A moment later the engine roared and then merged with the more distant traffic noise out on the road. Caroline sat doodling on the blotter, but there were angry spots of colour on her cheeks.

"I think I'll make myself a cup of hot milk," Laura murmured awkwardly. "Can I get you anything?"

"No, thank you."

The kitchen was warm and dark, hung about with memories of the evening meal. The pungent smell of the crabs rose from their empty shells in the bin and the sweet, strong fragrance of the strawberries still clung to the discarded baskets. As Laura measured milk into a saucepan, her tired mind went back over the momentous happenings of the day, Lewis's account of the events leading up to Noel's death and, later, to Clive Sandilands'.

She shivered, watching the warm milk begin to cream round the edges of the pan. She had told Paul she felt partly responsible for Sandilands' death before; now, guilt lay heavily upon her. But there was nothing to be gained by trying to apportion blame. Her destiny had already been entwined with that of Noel and Lewis and she was powerless even then to break the threads. The web of involvement went right back in time beyond the accident in which her mother was killed and which had been directly responsible for her coming to Four Winds. Even before that, the name of this house had been enough to send a cold prickle up her spine, as though her subconscious had always been aware of what lay in wait for her.

With a frothing rush the milk rose in a white flood and she snatched it off the flame and poured it into the mug. A little reluctantly she carried it back to the sitting-room. Although uncomfortably aware of Caroline's hostility, she had no wish for the moment to go to her room. Noel might be waiting for her and she hadn't the strength to deal with her yet. She was still perturbed by the pathological intensity of her jealousy towards Caroline that evening.

The French windows had been left open, but now the garden beyond them was dark and full of shadows. Caroline still sat in her little pool of lamplight, head bent over

188

the desk as she wrote her weekly letter to her children at boarding school. Another month and they would be home for the summer holidays.

Laura dropped into the sofa and sipped the hot milk cautiously. Edward and Caroline, Richard and Gillian, Toby and Janet, Paul. All of them, in their own ways, concerned about her, anxious for her well-being, all of them powerless to help her. Had she the strength to help herself? Lewis, certainly, could not be depended on. Laura was in no doubt which of them he wanted.

Caroline said without turning, "I thought you wanted an early night?"

"Yes, I'll go up now. Shall I shut the windows?"

"If you like. I'll lock up in a few minutes, when I've finished writing to Helen."

"Give her my love." She moved across and pulled the glass doors shut, sliding the bolts into place.

"There's no need to draw the curtains. I shan't be long."

Laura stooped to retrieve the empty mug from the floor by the sofa and her dress brushed against the vase of flowers standing in the grate. They made an effective splash of bright colour against the biscuit-coloured stone of the fireplace. She bent forward and brushed the petals she had dislodged behind the vase.

"Good night, Caroline."

"Good night."

Edward and Caroline's door stood open as Laura passed, the counterpane neatly folded and the bed turned down invitingly by Mrs. Baines. She reached her own room and slowly started to undress. The tiredness which had attacked her downstairs was now so powerful she could scarcely drag her feet across the floor. At last she was able to let herself drop on the bed and thankfully close

189

her eyes.

She must have slept, but suddenly she was wide awake. The moon poured a silver cascade of light onto the bed, bleaching the rose pink blankets to pearly grey. Without warning, she was gripped by fierce, choking rage which pumped through her like adrenalin as her mind fumbled helplessly to remember what had so upset her.

Caroline. Caroline and Lewis. A series of still pictures flicked through her head: Lewis leaning into Caroline's car when he first arrived, his hand possessively on her arm, and the two of them at dinner, acutely conscious of each other and of her not at all. What right had Caroline, with her own husband and children, to encroach on Lewis, who was and always had been hers alone? She must be taught a lesson.

She raised her head suddenly, remembering another picture the evening had left imprinted on her mind: the huge vase of flowers, the hearth where the splashes of fallen petals lay, and the brush she had used to sweep them away and then replaced beside the poker.

Without being aware of movement, her hands were turning the doorknob. Beyond, the sleeping house lay bathed in the silver light which streamed through its uncurtained windows. Edward was away. Caroline was alone.

On soundless feet she almost floated down the wide staircase. The moonlight was sufficient for her to see the dark shapes lying where she had left them in the hearth. The chrome handle of the poker was cold to her sleep-warmed hand. She gripped it, balanced it, and started back up the stairs filled with the excitement of revenge. Lewis had betrayed her, but Caroline's seductive glances were to blame.

Caroline's door was shut now, but it opened silently beneath her fingers and at last she was standing by the bed looking down at her as she lay sleeping, the glorious colour drained from her hair by the half-darkness. Caroline—

But Edward—what would he say when he returned tomorrow?

Hurry—don't hesitate now! It needn't be too hard a blow—just one satisfying swipe on that beautiful, complacently sleeping face.

But surely, didn't Lewis say—?

Lewis will understand. Hit her now, quickly, before she wakes!

No! No, Noel! Stop it! For God's sake, wait! He told me to tell you—

Hit her! Hit her!

No! She gave a sharp, distressed little cry as she wrestled with the force that was threatening to overpower her. Noel, listen! There's nothing between them—not any more! Really! He told me to tell you!

Nothing? But—I saw them!

Shaking violently in every limb, she seized the opportunity of Noel's sudden uncertainty to regain control, gazing with growing horror from the weapon in her hand to her still-sleeping sister-in-law. Dear God, what was she doing?

The poker slipped in her nerveless fingers and she grabbed frantically for it before it could fall with a thud and wake Caroline. She just managed to catch hold of it, but it was slipping about now in the sweat on her palms. In fact, sweat was cascading down her whole body in cold rivulets and still the convulsive shaking rattled every bone. She thrust her tongue between her chattering teeth to still their noise, and the blood spurted hotly.

Stumblingly she turned and fled back down the wide stairs, dropping the poker into place with a clatter she was sure must rouse the house and wiping her sticky hands down her nightdress as though Caroline's blood was indeed on them. Then, from one second to the next, her desperate energy drained away and she almost fell. Inch by inch she went back up the endless staircase, dragging herself by the banisters while tears of weakness and fright mingled with the sweat on her face. It seemed an eternity before she reached her room. She sank down beside the bed, arms spread over it in helpless supplication, and gradually the horrible spasms which were tormenting her lessened and she was able to haul herself up onto the bed.

Noel, you might have killed her! *I* might have killed her! And the sullen, half-frightened response: You should have told me. She put a hand across her eyes to press down the lids and will sleep to come and blot out the memory of what had happened. If Noel was as strong as this, what hope had she of ever escaping her?

Chapter 14

THE FOLLOWING day, Laura was limp and weak with a raging fever. Dr. MacIntyre, summoned hastily by Caroline, diagnosed a virus infection which, Laura thought with hysterical inner laughter, was a new way to describe Noel. There were medicines and pills to be taken almost hourly, and everyone assured her she would be feeling much better soon. But would she, or would she finally topple over the edge of normality into the waiting abyss of Noel? And, if this should happen, would she even be aware of it? Would anyone else, except Lewis? Noel was certainly clever enough to adapt slightly, to mask the period of transition by adopting some of Laura's own mannerisms so that she herself would remain undetected.

Throughout the day she lay back on her pillows, too spent to lift a hand unnecessarily and periodically drenched with weakening sweat. She could hardly bear to look at Caroline, who anxiously brought her a succession of cold drinks, obviously at a loss to understand the suddenness of the attack or the apparent agitation her own presence seemed to bring.

Eventually, with evident pangs of conscience, Caroline sat down beside the bed and began diffidently, "Laura, I hope you didn't put too much importance on the rather stupid way Lewis and I were behaving last night."

Laura bit her lip and turned her head away, and Caroline, thinking she had found at least one source of her

193

sister-in-law's distress, went on awkwardly, "It was only a kind of game, you know. After all, when you've been married for sixteen years or so, it's rather a temptation to find out if you're still attractive to other men."

She paused and Laura said dully, "It's nothing to do with me."

"Isn't it? I seemed to get the impression that you're becoming rather fond of him yourself."

Laura flushed painfully. "No."

"Was it because of Edward, then? I promise you I've no intention of running off and leaving him!" She waited for Laura's answering smile and when it didn't come, thankfully changed the subject. "By the way, Paul Denver phoned after lunch, but when I looked in, you were asleep. He was very sorry to hear you're ill and will phone again tomorrow."

"Thank you."

"I—can't help feeling that he's a much more suitable companion for you than Lewis, you know."

"I thought you didn't like him."

"Well, perhaps I was rather hasty. He doesn't like me, and I dare say that influenced me. But Edward gives him a lot of time and he seems genuinely fond of you. On the other hand, I don't think Lewis is capable of feeling deeply about anyone. He can be bitter and cynical and of course he's much too old for you. Also—"

"Yes?" Laura looked up at her defiantly.

"Well, there are other things, aren't there?" Her colour deepened. "All that precognition or whatever it was. If you ask me, it's not healthy. It would be much better not to get too involved with him."

"What about the book?"

"Haven't you just about all the information you need now?"

"I suppose so, more or less."

"In the future," Caroline said firmly, standing up, "I think you'd be much better advised to stick to historical novels." The door closed behind her and Laura smiled faintly. Poor Caroline, she obviously didn't fancy the idea of Lewis as a brother-in-law.

The sound of the front door reached her, and Edward's voice in the hall. A few minutes later he tapped on the door and came over to the bed, staring down at her with an anxious frown.

"Whatever brought this on, Laura? Toby and Janet were just saying how much better you seemed."

"The doctor says it's an infection of some sort." She felt a sudden rush of warmth for him, so solid, so dependable and so genuinely concerned about her. She turned her hand palm up on the counterpane and he accepted the silent invitation by sitting down and taking hold of it.

"How did the dinner go?"

"The food wasn't too bad, but there were the usual long, boring speeches afterwards. I didn't get back to Toby's till after one—he'd given me a key, of course—and then young Lucy woke screaming about five, so all in all it wasn't a very good night! But what about you? When did this start?"

"In the night. It wasn't a good one for me, either."

"I believe Lewis was here for dinner?"

"Yes."

"Laura—"

"Caroline's just warned me not to have so much to do with him, but it was all your idea, you know, in the first place."

"I didn't know what I was letting us all in for," Edward said grimly. "I didn't really know him very well before, but I can't say that I'm very impressed with him on closer acquaintance. Anyway, I suppose it's good of him to help you as he has and it won't be going on much longer, will it, once you've finished the book. Which reminds me, there was another letter from Fenella Gray this morning." His hand tightened on hers as the uncontrollable shudder ran through her. In Noel's absence, Lewis's confession of Clive Sandilands' murder seemed grotesque, unbelievable. If only she could tell Edward—

"I know Clive's death upset you," he was saying gently, "but Fenella's adjusting quite well to being on her own. The book is nearly finished. She sent you her best wishes and wants to know how yours is coming along. Will you drop her a line?"

She said in a choked voice, "If I hadn't wanted to hear about his work, he wouldn't have invited us for dinner, or—" spoken about Noel's death in front of Lewis, which was what had really sealed his fate.

"Laura, you must stop blaming yourself. It was just one of those terrible, senseless things which unfortunately happen all too often." He patted her hand and stood up. "Caroline said dinner was nearly ready so I'd better go down. She also asked me to remind you that it's time for your pills. Do you have a drink with them?"

He handed her the glass and the brightly coloured capsules and Laura meekly took them. They couldn't possibly do the slightest good, but they were unlikely to harm her and at least they reassured Edward and Caroline.

By the next day, as they had all so glibly prophesied, Laura had recovered sufficiently to go downstairs, and gradually her strength returned, but from that day forward she was in no doubt of the power which Noel could exercise over her if she chose.

Lewis still came to Four Winds most evenings, but Edward's cordiality was noticeably strained and Caroline usually found things to do elsewhere while he was there. Gradually and against her conscious will, Laura found herself growing closer to Lewis and she no longer had the strength to resist. It was as though she had summoned all her reserves to combat Noel's desire to injure Caroline and having used them up, she had been unable to build up any more.

Noel came and went as she chose, though she usually confined her possession to Lewis's visits. One evening, when Laura had been more successful than usual in fighting her off, she made her presence felt more definitely than ever before, materializing in a thick, cold mist which flowed towards Laura as she cowered on the bed, filling her eyes, her nose and her mouth with suffocating vapour until she was blinded and gasping for breath. Then, abruptly, the mist dispersed and she came to with a terrifying sense of strangeness. She flung herself off the bed with some half-formed intention of rushing in to Edward, but she was halted in mid-flight by a glimpse of her reflection in the mirror across the room.

In dazed disbelief her hands went up to her face, the fingers moving in shrinking fear over unfamiliar features, and as her stumbling feet drew her nearer to the glass, it was with a despairing sense of inevitability that she saw Noel's serene, triumphant face staring back at her.

It was soon after that incident that Laura suddenly decided to change her hair style, sweeping the fine hair away from her face and up into a smooth French pleat. It changed her appearance considerably, making her seem older, sleeker, altogether more poised. The impact on Lewis was immediate. He stood staring at her as she walked across the grass to join him, his eyes burning in the sudden sallowness of his face, and as she reached him, he took hold of both her hands, crushing them in his as his eyes raked endlessly over her face.

"Hi, Lew!" she said softly.

Paul, however, disapproved very strongly of Laura's changed appearance. "What have you done to yourself?" he demanded angrily. "You look ten years older!"

"I'm sorry if you don't like it," she replied primly.

"Too right I don't! What's come over you, Laura? You're not yourself at all!"

Indeed she was not. Paul started the car with a jerk and they drove in silence along the country lanes beyond Brocklehurst. After a while he said abruptly, "Term ends in another couple of weeks. My family expects me to go up north."

She looked at him, aware of a pang at the thought of his going away. "I'll miss you, Paul."

"Will you? I wish I could believe that. Look, it's no good, I've got to ask. Just what is there between you and Lewis Castleton?"

She twisted her hands on her lap. "I'm writing his biography. You know that."

Paul swerved to a halt and swivelled in his seat to face her. "Look, love, that answer may sound reasonable to you, but it's not good enough for me. I remember only too well how you reacted the first time you saw him. Shall I tell you what I think? I think he's trying to turn you into a replica of someone he once knew. All right, it sounds insane, I know, but—God, Laura, I lie awake night after night thinking about it."

She sat without moving, staring straight ahead.

"Haven't you anything to say to that?"

"Only that it would be better for you not to waste your

198

time thinking about me," she answered in a low voice. He reached out and very gently began to pull the pins from her hair until it fell loose about her face again in a soft cloud.

"That's better," he said quietly. "I only wish it was as easy to undo everything else. I know you made me promise not to say anything about those conversations we had, the atmosphere you felt in the house, and so on, but I really don't feel justified in keeping quiet any longer. I'm asking you to release me from that promise. Will you, Laura?"

She turned then to look at him. He was staring at her with an expression of helpless, rather angry vulnerability in his eyes and her heart ached for him.

"No," she said softly. "I'm sorry, but no."

"But I can't go off to Huddersfield leaving you in this condition! Heaven knows what might happen while I'm away."

"There's nothing you can do, Paul." She looked down at the pile of hairpins in her lap. "I can always pin up my hair again. Anyway that's only an 'outward and visible sign of an inward and spiritual—' "

"Not 'grace,' " he interrupted grimly. " 'Evil' would be more appropriate."

"Not evil either, really."

"So there is something?"

"Between Lewis and me? Yes, there's certainly something."

His voice was harsh. "Is he trying to make out he's in love with you?"

"In a way, I suppose."

"And what about you?"

She looked at him helplessly, knowing he couldn't be

expected to accept it as she must. "I need him, Paul." And, at the spasm of hurt which crossed his face, she added inadequately, "I'm sorry."

He moved fractionally away from her. "I seem to have been making rather a fool of myself," he said stiffly. "I beg your pardon. I'd better take you home."

Her eyes brimmed suddenly. "You will write, won't you, while you're away?"

"There doesn't seem to be much point."

"Please!"

"God, Laura, what are you trying to do to me? If you want Castleton, at least let me go!"

"I'm sorry, I'm being very stupid." A feeling of desolation lapped over her. What would she do if Paul abandoned her? If she lost him— Noel, losing interest, slipped away and in the same moment Paul turned his head.

"Well, don't *cry!*" he said roughly. "All right, I admit even that long-distance contact would be better than nothing. I'll write." Gently his fingers wiped away the tears on her cheek. "Okay?"

She nodded and tried to smile. He drew in his breath sharply and with a sudden movement pulled her into his arms and started to kiss her, deeply but tenderly. Clinging to him, she felt confusedly that she had come home after a long and dangerous journey. But that, of course, was an illusion. This was just a temporary respite which Noel had carelessly granted her. She had no right to let Paul think there was any chance for him.

Sensing her hesitant withdrawal, he released her, looking down at her with a shaky laugh. "Well, that's put my cards on the table in no uncertain manner! I presume I need hardly say I hadn't intended that to happen."

She sat up and he watched her anxiously. "Laura, you must have known for some time how I felt about you. know I'm not much of a catch, but I think I could make you happy. Won't you give me the chance?"

She shook her head. "I can't, Paul; it's simply not possible. Please don't ask me."

"But surely—"

"No!" In rising panic, her hands flew up to her head. "No, no, no!"

When at last she could look at him, his eyes had changed and hardened.

"Then it seems I owe you another apology. Obviously it's my day for making a nuisance of myself." A muscle jerked at the corner of his mouth. "Are you going to marry Castleton?"

Her heart gave a painful twist. She heard herself reply, "I suppose so."

"You don't sound exactly delirious with joy at the prospect." She didn't answer and he added flatly, "There's nothing I can do to change your mind?"

"It isn't my mind, Paul."

"What do you mean?" His voice was sharp and she pulled herself together hastily. She had answered him without thinking.

"Nothing." Slowly her hands went up to her hair and began to twist it back into place. He watched her with a kind of dull misery. When she had finished, she said quietly, "Thank you, Paul. For everything."

"I don't seem to have done anything except upset you."

This parting seemed frighteningly final. She said tentatively, "Will I see you again before you go up north?"

"I shouldn't think so. I imagine it would be better for both of us if I kept away. Are you sure you still want me to write?"

"Yes, please."

"Very well." He started the car, turned it in the narrow lane and they drove slowly back. Already she felt as if he had gone from her, and was filled with an overwhelming sense of bereavement. He seemed suddenly incredibly dear to her and at the same time completely inaccessible. He dropped her at the gate of Four Winds and they exchanged a few embarrassed phrases before he drove off. Laura was painfully aware of the tears which now streamed unchecked down her cheeks. She even started, futilely, to run after him, but it was too late and his car was already out of sight. Those few steps had taken her beyond the gateway and she went on walking, scarcely knowing what she was doing, down the hill into Brocklehurst village, silent and deserted on half-day closing. Wednesday afternoons with Paul had been a pleasurable landmark for her. Now they would have no meaning. Her footsteps quickened as subconsciously she went to meet Lewis.

She was almost running by the time she emerged on the far side of the village and turned into the lane leading to Gillet's cottage. The day was cooler than average, with low clouds and the sun had never broken through. Shivering in her thin dress, she pushed open the door without stopping to knock, finding herself directly in the small living-room. Lewis was sitting at the desk. He didn't seem surprised to see her.

"Hello, darling." He held out his hand and she went over to him, standing close behind him and looking over his shoulder at the notes he was making.

"Still working on the seaside resorts?"

"It's a long series! I've covered quite a lot of ground

since our day in Eastbourne. Just hang on for a moment, will you, while I finish this passage."

"Surely." She moved away, conscious of Noel and almost welcoming her, since it blotted out the pain of her parting from Paul. She noted approvingly that the photograph which had been removed from the scrapbook was now framed and standing on the desk. The hair style in the photograph was identical with the one she now wore and even the dress, more tailored than Laura's usual choice, was similar. She smoothed it down with a feeling of satisfaction. Despite Paul's disapproval, she had much more of an air about her now and the knowledge gave her confidence.

She glanced over at Lewis to find him watching her with a smile.

"What's so funny?"

"You, my love! You're prinking and preening like a peacock!"

"I was only thinking my appearance has improved lately."

"Indeed it has! The little English ugly duckling has changed into my beautiful American swan!"

Paul's uneasy words echoed in her head and to drown them she said quickly, "Are you nearly through? Shall I fix some coffee?"

Lewis drew in his breath. "Oh, Noel! Laura would have suggested tea!"

"I'll make tea if you'd rather."

"No, of course not. Have you any idea what it means to me to have found you again?"

She went to him quickly and his arm came round her.

"You're not frightened any more?" she asked anxiously.

"How can I be frightened of a real, flesh-and-blood woman?"

She had been right, then! She felt a thrust of triumphant excitement. Now that she had rid herself of the inopportune Paul, there was nothing to stand in her way. She rested her cheek momentarily on his dark head, and as she did so, something in one of the small drawers inside the desk caught her eye. It was a small silver powder compact. Lewis was completely still as she turned it towards the grey light from the window to read the inscription: "Noel—Lewis—Always."

The blood was thundering in her ears and behind her eyes. When had she last held this? She began to tremble and Lewis's arm held her fast.

"Remember when you handed me this?" She swayed a little and he repeated urgently, "Do you, Noel?"

Her tongue was dry and burning. "I think so."

"Tell me!"

She struggled to free herself. "Lewis—let me go!"

"Tell me!"

"It was that last night, wasn't it?" Her voice seemed to hum in her ears, far away and singsong. His laboured breathing shuddered through the stillness and she noticed detachedly the beads of perspiration on his face.

"Go on."

She stared down at the little compact and the disjointed memory came to her of a visit to a fortuneteller once who had held some object belonging to her and received vibrations from it. She said haltingly, "It's hard to remember— I was so sick and dizzy—"

"Think, Noel, think! It's vital that you should remember this!"

Another tremor shook her violently, rattling her teeth. "We were crossing to the car and a speck of dust blew in your eye. I felt in my purse and handed it to you so you could use the mirror to remove it."

He said almost to himself, "Laura could never have known that." He laughed suddenly and the sound was somehow shocking, making her flinch. "I must have slipped it into my pocket without thinking. Just as well— if I'd given it back to you, it might possibly have withstood the flames and then the fat would have been in the fire."

Mesmerized, her eyes went back to the inscription. "Yes, it's all there, isn't it? May I keep it now?"

"Of course."

Still moving in a dream, she dropped the compact into the open handbag on the chair. His hands dug into her shoulders as they turned her back to face him. "Noel—my love—"

But suddenly, frantically, Laura was struggling through, twisting herself away from his hold. He gazed at her blankly, uncomprehendingly, as she fought to retain her grasp on her own personality.

"She's gone!" she gasped. "Oh, Lewis, I thought I wasn't going to be able to get back! I—needed to see you—myself. I let her come because I was—miserable, but it—was too much."

"Yes," he agreed tonelessly after a minute, "it was too much. Poor little Laura. Sit down and tell me why you were miserable."

Shakily she let him lead her to a chair and sank down into it. "I was with Paul."

"I see. Did he upset you?"

"We upset each other."

He was watching her keenly. "I was right, wasn't I? He is in love with you."

"Yes."

"And you told him he hadn't a hope?"

Her eyes filled again. "More or less."

He patted her hand. "Never mind, sweetheart, he'll get over it."

She said slowly, "You tend to belittle everyone's love except your own, don't you, Lewis?"

"Do I? Perhaps. But I did admit that even my love had become a little muted as time passed."

"Yes. It was when you said that, that Noel really started pushing to get back to you."

"In any case I was wrong. It hadn't faded, it was just lying dormant. I love her—you—as much as I ever did."

She said quietly, "You don't love me at all, Lewis, and I don't love you. I told you that. What's more, I'm becoming more and more convinced that I love Paul, after all."

"Nonsense!" His voice was firm and authoritative. He pulled her to her feet and into his arms, holding her gently, his fingers caressing the back of her neck. "One thing you must get completely clear, Laura. I do love you, and not only because you give me Noel back. And you love me, however much you may fight against it. You know that, don't you?"

She looked up at him, troubled and confused. His face just above hers was exactly as it had been in her dream those long months ago—hooded, slate-grey eyes, broad nose, self-indulgent mouth and the dark hair falling over his forehead. She sighed a little, too worn-out to fight his strength combined with Noel's.

"Don't you, Laura?" he persisted.

"Yes, Lewis, I suppose I do."

And as his face came down towards her, she let herself be swept away again, tacitly relinquishing her body to the powerful resurgence of the ebullient Noel.

Chapter 15

JULY slipped past. Robert and Helen returned from school and presumably Paul travelled north to Yorkshire; Laura had not heard from him again. Suddenly, all the talk at Four Winds was of "the holiday."

"What holiday?" Laura enquired at last, and they all looked at her incredulously.

"*Our* holiday, of course! In Italy!"

"But—I don't know anything about it—"

Edward regarded her smilingly. "My dearest Laura, you must have been in a world of your own these last few weeks!"

"I vaguely heard you mention holidays, but I just thought you meant when the children came home."

"In that case," Caroline remarked, "you'd better have a quick look through your wardrobe to make sure you have everything you need. We go a week on Friday."

"But—I can't go!" She stared at them, panic-stricken.

"Might I ask why not?" Edward enquired.

I can't leave Lewis! The words were in her head but she managed to hold them back. "Well, I—you don't want me there all the time."

"Of course we want you, and what's more we've no intention whatever of going without you, so you can forget that."

"Fancy not wanting to go to Italy!" Robert said wonderingly.

"Could you tell me something more about it, then?"

"Of course. We rent a villa on the Adriatic coast. You must have heard about it before, we've been there for the last two years. It's a lovely spot within easy reach of Venice without all the rowdy tourism you get if you're too near. We lie on the beach all day on a diet of fruit and cheese, and have a slap-up meal in the local *ristorante* every evening. It suits us perfectly."

Later, when she found Edward alone with the evening paper, Laura said tentatively, "You know, I'm really not at all sure that I want to go to Italy, Edward."

"Oh, Laura, really! It will just put the finishing touch to your recovery, I'm sure. You might even meet a handsome gondolier!"

She smiled dutifully but her eyes were troubled. He said more seriously, "It's Lewis, isn't it? Surely you can bear to leave him for three weeks!"

She flushed. "I suppose you think I'm very stupid."

"Are you sure you know what you're doing, love? If you've really set your heart on him and he feels the same, I suppose I'll just have to accept it, but—I don't know. There's something about him I'm not happy about, though I can't really put my finger on it. And even allowing for love's young dream, there is something a bit—obsessive about your attitude to each other. Frankly, I think it will do you good to get away from him for a while. You might even feel differently by the time you get back."

"I shouldn't count on that," she answered with quiet fatalism.

"What about young Denver? Has he bitten the dust completely?"

She held down the surge of unhappiness which rose inside her and replied almost steadily, "There was never really anything between Paul and me."

"Not for want of trying on his part, I imagine."

"Please, Edward!"

"All right. Well, Lewis or no Lewis, you're coming to Italy with us, my girl, and he can like it or lump it!"

"I'd better go and tell him," she said quietly.

"Can't you phone?"

"No, I've some papers to return to him anyway."

In the warm enclosure of the garden at Gillet's cottage, Lewis listened carefully to what she had to say. "Do you want to go, darling?"

"I don't want to leave you."

His fingers were tight on hers. "I shall miss you every second of every day."

"I suppose we have come to the end of the collaboration on the book, anyway."

"You think you've finished with me then, do you?" he asked teasingly. "You won't get rid of me as easily as that!"

"But we haven't any—reason—" she had almost said "excuse"—"to see each other so often now."

"I imagined," he said softly, "that we had the best reason in the world."

"Lewis—"

"Who are you today, sweetheart? You're so alike now, I'm not always sure!"

An apprehensive tremor lifted the hairs on the back of her neck. It was true. She too was finding it increasingly difficult to detect Noel's presence. Slowly, insidiously, Noel's infatuation with Lewis was seeping into her own consciousness, making her restive when she was away from him. Only occasionally, when Paul's name was mentioned, did she feel a stab of the remembered pain.

She leant her head against Lewis's shoulder and his lips

moved over her hair. He loved her. It was all right. Somehow they would live through the three weeks without each other, and perhaps, when she came back, he would mention marriage again. This time, she knew, she would not resist. There was no point any longer in imagining she had any life without him.

The next morning's post brought a letter from Paul. The writing was unfamiliar, a black, forceful scrawl, but the Huddersfield postmark was identification enough and her treacherous heart gave a little jump. She tore open the envelope at once, standing in the hall, her eyes flying down the closely written pages. He began "Dear Laura" and ended "Yours, Paul." In between was news of his family and his home, the books he was reading, the films he had seen. Illogically she felt flat, let down. She folded the letter neatly and put it back in its envelope. Since it had been she who had asked him to write, she must reply before they went away and let him know their holiday address. Thoughtfully, she went in to breakfast.

It was three days before they were due to go to Italy that Richard phoned. The telephone rang as they were going through to dinner, and Caroline stopped in the hall to answer it. A moment later she came to the dining-room door, flushed and tight-lipped.

"Edward, will you come and speak to Richard? He's got some ridiculous idea of coming to Italy with us, and nothing I say makes any difference."

Edward pushed back his chair. "He wants to come? But that's splendid! Why on earth shouldn't he? Heaven knows when we last had a holiday altogether."

Caroline said tightly, "It's out of the question. You'll see that if you just think for a moment. For one thing there aren't enough bedrooms and he'll expect to bring—that girl." Her colour deepened and her eyes went guardedly to the children.

"I can sleep on the sofa in the living-room," Robert volunteered eagerly. "Richard can have my bed!" Richard had long ago refused point-blank to be called "Uncle," a stand which still rankled with the conventional Caroline.

Edward was already in the hall. Caroline sat down at the table and her eyes went resentfully to Laura. "No doubt you'd be only too delighted to have them, too."

"Yes, I would. I know it will mean extra work, but you'll have me to help you this year, and I'm sure Gillian would too."

"Gillian!" said Caroline contemptuously.

"What's she like," Helen asked curiously, "Richard's new girl friend?"

Caroline bit her lip and it was left to Laura to answer tactfully, "Very nice. You've probably seen her on TV."

There was a clamour of interest from the children. "What's her name? Gillian Marlowe? Yes, she was in 'The Persuaders' once. And the Herries series which Mummy watched on BBC 2."

"That was before she became friendly with Richard," Caroline said defensively. Helen dropped her fork and flew out of the room before her mother could stop her. Her voice reached them clearly.

"Daddy, they are coming, aren't they? Gillian Marlowe too?"

Caroline called angrily, "Helen! Come here at once and eat your meal!"

The child came back dutifully and resumed her place. "I'll be able to get her autograph for all my friends," she remarked with satisfaction. "Richard always knows such *interesting* people!"

"What did you tell him?" Caroline demanded, as Edward also, returned to the table.

"We could hardly say no, could we? Anyway, the more the merrier."

Caroline did not reply, but later, when the children had gone to bed, she returned to the attack. "Surely you can see that it's most unsuitable for Richard to bring that woman? It was bad enough when they came here for the weekend, but fortunately Peter's too young to notice that kind of thing. But Robert and Helen—"

"Relax, darling, he's promised to be the soul of discretion. We'll have to shuffle the bedrooms about a bit, but there'll be nothing untoward, don't worry."

"How many bedrooms are there at the villa?" Laura asked.

"Three, two double and a single. Normally the boys share a room and Helen has the little one. There's also a pile of camp beds, but we've never needed them before."

"And how," demanded Caroline, "do you propose to reshuffle?"

"Simple. Laura and Gillian can have the boys' room, with Helen on a camp bed in the corner. We'll have Peter in with us, Richard can have Helen's room and Robert, as he said, can sleep on the sofa."

"It'll be like a doss house!" Caroline said disgustedly.

"Nonsense! We're hardly there anyway, only to sleep."

Edward smiled across at Laura. "Richard will have a pleasant surprise when he sees you. You're like a different person!"

The coffee cup she was holding rattled on its saucer and she hastily replaced it on the low table. "Yes," she answered quietly, "I suppose I am."

212

The villa was painted strawberry pink. It had a riot of oleanders in its tiny garden and beyond the gate the ground fell away to shingle leading to the beach. Inside, it was cool and airy with stone floors and brightly painted shutters to all the windows.

"Isn't it fabulous," Gillian commented, "that they actually have to try to keep the heat *out!*"

Laura laughed and agreed. Since leaving England, she had been aware of a soaring of the spirits. Noel, having lost the battle against her going away, had let her go in peace. Perhaps she herself remained with Lewis. It didn't seem to matter. For the next three weeks she was free to relax with her family, and she was unequivocally grateful.

The days passed as Edward had foretold—days full of sand, sea and hot sunshine. They all lived in their swimsuits, their skins turning deep brown. Even Laura, who normally did not tan easily, acquired a lovely rich colour, and only the red-haired Gillian lamented her misfortune in having to stay under the beach umbrella for most of the day. Her thin bird-like body was even more minute in the skimpy bikini she wore and her arms, shoulders and face were liberally spattered with a peppering of freckles.

"And how's my favourite sister?" Richard enquired lazily during the first week. "You're blossoming into quite a dish, my love!"

"Thank you kindly, sir!"

"That hair-do suits you. I should think it's cool, too, in this heat."

"But it makes her look a lot older," Gillian remarked, rubbing the suntan oil along his smooth brown back.

"Different, certainly. How's the magnum opus progressing?"

"All right." She didn't want to think about it, but added perforce, "All the preliminary work is finished now, so I'm ready to start writing in earnest."

"And did this fellow whatever his name is have as interesting a life as you hoped?"

"Yes, indeed. What about you? Any new plays on the stocks?"

"A couple, yes. One commissioned for a TV series, another for a single play slot. I'm going to have a shot at producing the single."

"So he won't have his precious dialogue mucked about!" Gillian said with a laugh, settling down beside him. "There was a ding-dong battle over the last one!"

"I remember, it was when I was staying with you. I did enjoy that couple of weeks, even though I was feeling so groggy."

"But not enough, apparently, to come back when invited," Richard remarked, opening one eye to look at her reproachfully.

"I couldn't at that particular point. I'd just decided on the book."

"Well, now you've reached a pause, how about coming back with us straight from here? We'd love to have you, wouldn't we, Gillie?"

"Of course we would."

"It's sweet of you, but by the time we get back, I'll have been away long enough for the moment."

"It's a shame we haven't more room at the flat. I have the feeling you'd be better off with us than with the worthy Edward and his good lady!"

Laura smiled a little guiltily. "They've been very good to me."

"Caroline too?" Richard enquired with raised eyebrow.

214

"Certainly. I know you don't like her—"

"Really? I hoped I'd managed to conceal the fact. God, she puts years on me! Expects every man within range to pay her homage. It wouldn't wash with me and she's never forgiven me!"

"Oh, Richard!" Laura protested laughingly. "She's not that bad!"

"As hard as nails too," Richard continued imperturbably. "Every time I see her I have a regrettable urge to try to shock her!"

"If it's any comfort, you nearly always succeed!"

"How gratifying! Oh, Laurie!" He reached out for her hand. "You don't know how good it is to have this kind of conversation with you again—just like old times. Last time I saw you at Four Winds, you were so up-tight I could hardly get near you, and dear Caroline put the fear of God into me with wild talk about dreams and portents and Lord knows what else. That's why I did my damnedest to get you to come back with us." He laughed. "What a lot of moonshine it seems now!"

She returned the pressure of his fingers and did not reply. These few weeks were too precious to spoil with doubts and conjectures. If only she need never go back! She pulled herself up sharply. Not go back to Lewis? And to underline her perfidy, it was at that moment that Edward, who had been to the village, appeared above her and dropped a letter onto her.

She sat up quickly, her fingers trembling as she tore it open. Unlike Paul, Lewis had begun uncompromisingly, "My darling—" She read through the letter with her heart thundering against her ribs. Seeing the words of love in black and white was like hearing them for the first time and as her eyes lingered over the tender, passionate phrases, she was filled once more with restless impatience to get back to him.

"Stop brooding, Laura!" Richard commanded, tugging her to her feet. "Gillie and I are going for a swim. Come and join us!"

She slipped the letter under her towel and ran down the beach with them, and as she ran, the impact of Lewis fell away again and receded into a past which, until it linked up with the future on her return to Brocklehurst, could for the time being be put out of mind.

The holiday was punctuated with such interludes. Laura's share of the post became a family joke. She had three letters from Paul while they were away, and six or seven from Lewis. The fact that no one else received any added to her embarrassment. And all Paul's began circumspectly, "Dear Laura." Several times she found herself wishing just a few of Lewis's extravagant words could overflow into Paul's unembellished prose, but she was quick to push such thoughts away. If she had responded differently in the car that day, she knew that Paul's letters would have been very different. She had only herself to blame. Somehow that knowledge brought little comfort.

The weeks slid into one another. They spent a day in Venice, another in Viareggio, but for the most part they slept and swam and ate. They stopped at the little shop each morning on the way to the beach to buy bottles of the local wine, long loaves, fruit and cheeses for their picnic lunch. The adults never wanted much to eat in the middle of the day, though the children's appetites were undiminished.

After lunch each day, Richard and Gillian returned to the villa for their siesta, allegedly because the midday sun was too strong for her fair skin and Richard was too gal-

lant to allow her to go back alone. That explanation pa-
tently satisfied the children, which was all that mattered,
but Laura was always uncomfortably aware of Caroline's
hard, resentful eyes following the two of them as they
wandered hand in hand up the shingle. They usually returned soon after three, and at five or six they would all
wander back in twos and threes, queuing for the shower.
It was only then that the women changed into dresses for
the evening meal which, Italian fashion, they ate about nine
o'clock. It was a long day for the children, especially
Peter, but since they slept a lot on the beach they were all
allowed to stay up with the others.

The evening meal was the time of the day that Laura
loved most, sitting outside the restaurant under the gay
awning while the exotic food was laid before them, hearing the laughter of their fellow diners and looking across
the square to the lights of the pavement cafés where other
holiday-makers, French, German and American, sat
drinking coffee or Campari-soda.

Sometimes her eyes would go slowly round their table,
imprinting the individual features of the family on her
mind as though this might be the last chance she had of
being with them: Edward, unusually tanned and relaxed
in his open-neck shirt; Richard, even more handsome with
his teeth flashing in his brown face; Caroline, beautiful but
a little withdrawn; Gillian, quiet and unobtrusive, never
far from Richard's side, and the three children: Helen,
whose puppy-fat was fining down in preparation for
young womanhood; Robert, tall and rather gawky; and
young Peter, intent as always on his food. Her heart
seemed to swell almost to bursting point with love for
them all. If only time could stand still, petrifying them
into this everlasting contentment. But against her chair lay

217

her handbag, containing the silver compact and the growing collection of love letters, symbols of that other life to which she had no option but to return.

At last the three weeks were up and it was time to pack for home. On the last day of August they reluctantly locked up the villa, clean, bare and impersonal once more, and piled into the two waiting taxis that were to take them to the airport. Edward and Caroline went in the first with the two younger children, Robert hanging back to go with Laura, Richard and Gillian in the second. During the holiday, Laura had become somewhat ruefully aware of Robert's passionate admiration for his debonair uncle, and his mother's furious resistance to it.

Several times, to the shared amusement of herself and Gillian, Robert had nonchalantly suggested that he and Richard should walk round the point to the next bay, or go on ahead of the others to the restaurant, or some other excuse to get him to himself. Richard, good-humoured as always and not unnaturally gratified by such obvious admiration, had complied, with a secret wink at the two girls, his enjoyment of the situation considerably enhanced by Caroline's silent resentment.

Now, in the taxi, the boy began diffidently, "Do you think it would be at all possible for me to come up to London and spend a few days with you before term starts? It would be great if I could go along to the TV studios with you one day. I've decided I want to write plays myself when I leave school."

Richard shot a wary look at Gillian, but she was answering pleasantly, "Of course you must come, if your parents will let you. There are all kinds of things we can show you, and I'm sure it could be arranged for you to watch some rehearsals for Richard's play."

218

"Gosh!" Robert turned his radiant face towards her. "That would be just groovy! Are you in it?"

Gillian laughed. "I'm in one of them, yes."

Laura reflected that Gillian was much more natural and forthcoming away from the aura of Caroline. She wondered if she shared Richard's dislike of his sister-in-law or merely felt uncomfortable in face of her unyielding disapproval.

"We don't want Helen, of course," Robert said firmly. "She'll probably want to come, but she'd only get in the way."

"She could always come another time if she'd like to," Gillian said tactfully.

The taxi swung off the road, taking the turning for the airport. Overhead, giant silver planes screamed in take-off.

"I bet it's raining in London!" Robert said gloomily.

Richard laughed. "Never mind, it's been a wonderful holiday, and all the rain in the world won't be able to wash away the memory of it."

Laura stumbled out of the taxi after Gillian. Her disinclination to return to Brocklehurst had returned in full force and she grasped at her brother's words to comfort her. At least she had the holiday to remember, the mental photograph of the circle of faces round the table.

"Come on, love!" Richard took her arm. "You look a bit shaky. Apprehensive about the flight? I can supply you with all the statistics about road accidents!"

She forced a smile. "Don't bother—I was in one of them, remember!"

Richard put a hand theatrically to his forehead. "How tactless can one be! It shows how much better you must be for me to have been able to forget it!"

Edward and Caroline were waiting with the children in

the departure lounge. Edward smiled across at Laura. "Glad you came after all?"

"Didn't she want to?" Richard turned to her in surprise.

"She wasn't at all sure. Too many commitments at home!"

Richard frowned slightly. "Time enough for those."

"We all know you don't believe in commitments, Richard," Caroline said shrewishly.

Richard, unabashed, glanced in her direction with malicious amusement. "Mi-aow!" he said deliberately, and she flushed and turned away. Their flight was called and they gathered their cases together, glad of the diversion to dispel the embarrassment.

It had indeed been a wonderful holiday, Laura reflected, a welcome respite from all the strains and stresses of the last months. But now it was over and she had to return, to Noel as well as to Lewis. Had she been able to build up enough strength for the renewed battles that awaited her? With a little tremble of foreboding, she went up the steps leading to the plane.

Chapter 16

NOEL was waiting for her, resentful and impatient. If Laura had hoped to build up her resistance during her absence in Italy, she soon realized that Noel had been engaged in much the same exercise and, as always, she proved the stronger. Despairingly, Laura began to feel the firm ground slipping away from beneath her as her mind swirled with the rush of thoughts and remembrances that were not her own.

Briefly, she considered taking up Richard's invitation and leaving Brocklehurst at once, but in her heart she knew it would be of no use. A temporary respite she had been unwillingly granted. Now there was to be no escape. Lewis and Noel would find her wherever she went. As the bleak realization came to her, she abruptly gave up the struggle, allowing herself to sink without further resistance into the waiting depths of Noel's personality.

Her sudden and complete surrender seemed to throw Noel off balance and, intoxicated at this proof of her power, she used it recklessly to indulge in recollections of people and places which had been important to her during her lifetime.

A nightmare existence began for Laura. Even going into Brocklehurst became an endurance test as the scene before her eyes shifted and changed constantly—at one moment a busy city street full of roaring traffic, at the next a deserted beach with stretches of white sand. The village itself seemed to have existence only in her own mind, but even when it materialized in its turn, it was as strange and alien as the other unknown places she glimpsed in these crazed flashes. Vaguely she remembered her first impression of the square houses as frumpy matrons, and now she could easily imagine them huddling together and tilting their chimneys to exchange malicious gossip—"There goes the mad girl from up at Four Winds."

As these hallucinations gained in clarity and frequency, so the normal, everyday life of Four Winds receded, giving way to superimposed images until Laura, groping blindly, had no way of knowing which was the reality.

Unlike the gradual possession which had preceded it, this sudden and rapid decline could hardly fail to be apparent to Edward and Caroline, and they reacted with stunned incredulity.

"Laura, what is it?" Edward demanded urgently one evening, holding onto her hand. "Caroline says you walked straight into the road today and it was only because the lorry was able to swerve up on the pavement that it managed to avoid you!"

She frowned with the effort of trying to understand what he was saying. Edward's face seemed to be hidden by a floating gauze curtain which obscured his features.

"I guess I just didn't see it. I was watching Clark take the salute."

"You were—? Who's Clark?" She heard his voice shake. "Laura dear, I want you to go and lie down quietly for a while. I'm going to ask Dr. MacIntrye to come and have a look at you."

She refocussed on his face with difficulty. It was drawn and frightened and she wondered helplessly how she could reassure him.

"I don't need a doctor, Edward. I'm not sick, just a little

222

confused."

"I know," he said gently, "but we have to get to the bottom of what's causing the confusion. You've been making such good progress all summer, and in Italy you were almost your old self again. It's hard to believe we've only been back just over a week, there's such a change in you. I'll be much happier for MacIntyre to see you."

She said quietly, "He won't be able to do anything."

"Of course he will!" Edward contradicted sharply. "He can give you tranquilizers and sedatives, and if they don't work, he can put us in touch with a specialist who—"

Laura sighed. "All right, I'll see him if it'll make you feel better."

The doctor called the next morning. He talked to her in his low, attractive voice as he examined her, and since Noel was carefully suppressing herself, she was able to reply to his questions clearly and calmly. When he had completed his examination, he sat back and looked at her gravely.

"Miss Hardy, you must know that your brother and sister-in-law are very concerned about you."

"Yes. I'm sorry."

"They've asked me to persuade you to spend a few days in a nursing home near here, where you can have specialized attention."

She held his eyes for a moment, then made up her mind. "Doctor, can I ask you something? Do you believe in psychic phenomena—spirits, ghosts, if you like, and the possibility of—possession?"

He drew a deep breath but his steady gaze never left her face. "That's quite a question! As a man of science I can only give you a qualified answer, though admittedly almost daily things are being scientifically proved that no one would have given credit to ten years ago."

" 'More things in heaven and earth'?"

"Exactly."

"You see, Doctor, there's nothing wrong with my mind. The trouble is that someone—something—else is trying to—take it over. Can you come anywhere near accepting that?"

"It does rather go beyond my sphere," he said slowly, "and as a medical man I've been trained to look for more concrete causes of mental disorder. On the other hand, I also know for a fact that in the last decade or so there has been a fantastic increase in requests for exorcism."

" 'Creature of water, creature of salt' and 'Satan and his fallen angels'—but you know I don't think that's the answer. The Church persists in regarding these spirits as demons of some kind, whereas I don't think she's an *evil* spirit at all, just a desperate one."

"She?"

"Noel Balfour. The girl who has possession of me."

"You actually know who she is?" He was leaning forward incredulously.

"Of course, I know everything about her. After all, part of the time I *am* Noel. There's another thing against exorcism, from my point of view." A tremor ran through her. "She's stronger than I am, Dr. MacIntyre. If any spirit was driven out, I'm sure it would be mine."

The doctor leant forward and covered her shaking hands with his. "I'd no idea things had gone as far as this. You must have help, and quickly. I'm not qualified to treat you myself, but I would urge you most strongly to go to Moorlands for a few days and put yourself in their hands."

She drew back. "I've heard of those places. If I go, I

224

may never be able to get out again."

"Of course you will," he said briskly. "You'd go in as a voluntary patient, either for treatment or just observation, and you'd be free to come out any time you wished."

"Lewis wouldn't like it."

"Who?"

"Lewis Castleton. He wants me to marry him. He was in love with Noel, so he's hardly likely to agree to her being driven away."

"My God!" MacIntyre said under his breath. "Miss Hardy, let me phone Moorlands now, please, and book you in as soon as they can take you."

His urgency reached her, but Noel, alarmed at this threat, clamped firmly over her mind.

"No, really, Doctor. I've tried to explain. I'm sorry if you can't accept my explanation, but I assure you I'm not ill and a nursing home would be no use at all. Thank you for your advice—I'm only sorry I can't take it."

He looked at her despairingly for a long moment then, with a helpless shrug, he left her. As soon as he'd gone, she slipped off the bed and opened the door again quietly. Edward had been waiting anxiously in the hall and his voice reached her.

"Would you like to come in here for a moment, Doctor?"

She stole out onto the landing and down the stairs. No one was about. Carefully she put her ear against the closed sitting-room door.

"To be honest," the doctor was saying, "this is hardly my province. Physically she's tense and run-down, but nothing to cause undue concern, but mentally—I don't know. She appears lucid and even rational, yet some of the things she said point strongly to schizophrenia."

225

"Oh, God!" Caroline's voice was high and shaking.

"But you said she seemed quite normal!" Edward broke in sharply.

"That's just the point. Schizophrenia is a personality split. One half would seem entirely normal, the other—well, it would depend."

"Is she *dangerous?*" Caroline demanded hysterically.

Laura moved away without waiting for his reply. She had been dangerous once, to Caroline; or rather, Noel had. Was she Noel? Split personality. It seemed a fair conclusion, though she herself knew it wasn't split but dual, two distinct and independent minds vying for position in one body.

It was suddenly imperative that she should see Lewis. She let herself soundlessly out of the house, keeping well over to the right of the drive, out of sight of the sitting-room windows. The warm September air touched her face, soothing her, as she hurried along the road trying to work out what had really happened that afternoon.

It had all been so clear at the time. They were at West Point and she was thinking how tall and strong Clark looked, with the sunlight glinting on his row of medals. How could a lorry suddenly have loomed up on the parade ground? No wonder she hadn't been expecting it.

Clark's picture filled her mind—the iron-grey, slightly curly hair, the straight, fierce eyebrows and clear, honest blue eyes. How could she desert him when he was badly wounded and needed her so much? Lewis must be made to understand.

The trees and village green of Brocklehurst quivered and wavered in front of her eyes like reflections in a deep pool of water ruffled by a passing wind. She must go to Lewis. She had no idea where she was, but somehow she

226

would find him. Laura, do go away and stop distracting me!

She began to run, stumbling along blindly, bumping into the rough stone walls, twisting her ankle on the uneven cobbles. Would he ever understand how hard it was for her to turn him away?

"Just one more evening together," he had said. And it really would have to be the last, because the plane had already left Saigon. She had refused to listen when Clark had warned her, all those years ago, that one day she might fall for someone nearer her own age. She had insisted, and implicitly believed, that he was all she would ever want. And, to be honest, her position as his wife had appealed to her strongly, with all the attendant respect and privileges. Clark Balfour was well-known and liked throughout the States long before the war in Vietnam had brought him world-wide fame, having distinguished himself in the Second World War under Eisenhower. And again, she had always considered herself too cool, too reserved ever to be passionately in love with anyone. How could she have known that when love finally came to her it would prove so strong, so indestructible as to transcend time and space and death itself?

Death? She stumbled to a halt, frowning and gasping for breath. Why had she suddenly thought of death? Because all at once she felt so strange and ill, and the steering wheel wouldn't respond under her hands.

Lewis— She couldn't turn her head to look at him, but in an intuitive flash, she knew he had no intention of helping her. Lewis!

The anguished cry, whether it was in her head or shouted aloud, jerked her spiralling attention back to the present and she found herself panting and dishevelled out-

227

side a tiny cottage. Wonderingly, she looked back along the way she had unknowingly come. With no recollection of how she had arrived here, she pushed feebly at the door in front of her and it swung open. And then all was well because somehow Lewis was here, had gathered her up with a low cry and carried her to the small leather sofa, rocking her in his arms. Somehow, incredibly, she had come home.

At one point during the hours that followed, the telephone sounded shrilly and he stretched out an arm to it.

"What? Yes, of course she's here! Where else would she be? What the hell have you been doing to her? No—" His voice sharpened. "Please don't. I'll bring her back myself when she's calmer. My God, Hardy, I've some things to say to you!"

He dropped the phone back on its hook, cutting off the stream of argument that was still coming over the wire, and she nestled back in his arms contentedly. Outside the diamond-paned windows the air was thickening bluely.

"Darling—" His breath was warm, and she lifted her face to it like a flower to the sun. "Could you manage a bowl of soup now if I get it for you?"

"Yes, I'd like that." She was empty and light-headed. When had she last eaten? At the motel? No, Edward—but who was Edward? She struggled through the wispy strands of confusion.

"Stay here, then." He slid her gently off his knee onto the comfortable, sagging leather cushions of the sofa. She lay back, her eyes going dreamily over the old rafters and the little wooden staircase leading to the room above where, in a different existence, she had helped Lewis hang some drapes.

228

A wedge of light lay across the floor from the open kitchen door behind her and she could hear the clinking of crockery as he prepared the meal.

Suddenly a name struck into her mind out of nowhere, echoing like a vibrating chord. Paul? She pushed herself into a sitting position, trying to pinpoint an elusive memory, but Lewis was dragging over the small table and setting down on it two steaming bowls of soup, some crusty bread and a glass of milk. She let the memory slip away again and began to sip the liquid, her eyes on Lewis's across the table.

"Better now, darling?"

She nodded cautiously.

"Enough for me to tell you something exciting?"

"Yes?" She laid down her spoon and waited expectantly.

"I've applied for a special licence. How about naming the day?"

"Licence?"

"Yes, my love, licence! Unfortunately we can't just walk into a registry office and demand to be married!"

Her mind jerked like an exposed nerve as Noel, delirious with joy, temporarily loosened her hold and, frightened and struggling, Laura fought her way to the surface.

"No, Lewis, I can't!" She jumped up and the table rocked, spilling the soup as he leant forward quickly to steady it.

"My dearest girl, you can and I sincerely trust you will!"

He came round and took hold of her arms. "Sweetheart, you're still upset. I shouldn't have mentioned it this evening."

She shivered violently under his hands, a tide of panic rising in her throat like nausea. "Take me home, please, Lewis."

"Of course, darling, of course." With his arm round her shoulders, he led her gently out to the car and they bumped their way along the lane to the main road.

"Don't let them frighten you, Noel," he said jerkily. "There's nothing they can do without your consent. That's another point in favour of our marrying as soon as possible. With a husband behind you, they won't stand a chance."

She shuddered uncontrollably. "A chance of what?"

"Of—sending you away for treatment of any sort."

They turned into the gateway of Four Winds, and immediately Edward came out of the house as though he'd been waiting and watching for the car. He pulled the door open before Lewis had properly stopped.

"Laura! Why ever did you go off like that without telling anyone? You had us all worried to death!"

"Why shouldn't she?" Lewis enquired tightly. "Is she a prisoner?"

"Don't be ridiculous." Edward was helping her from the car. "Are you all right, love? We were frightened out of our wits."

"I'm all right," she said through stiff lips. This slow progression to the front door with Edward holding her arm brought back an uneasy memory of her first arrival at Four Winds. But then Lewis hadn't been behind them. Or had he? Of course, Lewis had always been in the background. It was just that she hadn't then been aware of him.

Caroline was at the open door. "Is she all right?"

Laura smiled faintly and a spark of her old spirit asserted itself. "All right enough to answer for myself!" she retorted, and noted their surprise with satisfaction.

Edward had turned. "I'd rather you didn't come in just now, Castleton, if you don't mind. We need to devote all our time to Laura, and obviously your presence will complicate things."

Lewis stiffened. "Perhaps you should let—Laura"—he stumbled over the name—"decide whether or not she needs my support."

"Your support?" Edward repeated furiously. "My God, haven't you done enough? She was perfectly all right all the time we were in Italy, and as soon as she gets back to you, this happens. You can take your 'support,' as you call it, elsewhere."

"Just a moment, Hardy." The whiplash in Lewis's voice made Edward pause and turn back to him. "This may hardly be an auspicious moment to mention it, but it can hardly have escaped your notice that Laura and I love each other. We're going to be married as soon as it can be arranged."

Laura swayed a little and felt Edward's grip tighten on her arm as she registered the choked gasp that Caroline gave. And in the same instant Noel furiously reclaimed her, battling down her feeble attempts to escape from the net that was closing about her.

"Married?" Edward sounded dazed. "Laura, is this true?"

"Perfectly true," Noel answered steadily, and saw the flash of triumph in Lewis's eyes. As the rest of them stood unmoving, he bent forward and kissed her firmly on the mouth.

"Good night, darling; sleep well. I'll phone in the morning to see how you are. And don't be frightened. Everything's going to be all right." His eyes swept coldly over Edward and Caroline. "Good night."

He turned and walked quickly back to the car. Edward pulled Laura into the hall and slammed the door.

"Laura—sweetie, you can't! You don't really want to marry him?"

"But of course I do."

"He's twenty years older than you are!"

"Twenty-five," she corrected automatically. How often did she have to listen to that argument?

"But he's only forty-three," Caroline said shakily. "He—told me once."

Fool, they were talking about Lewis, not Clark, but he was only eight years older. It seemed pointless to argue with them.

"He's a very attractive man," she said instead. "Surely you agree, Caroline?"

Caroline shot her a startled glance. "Yes, yes, he is, but—"

"Well, one thing's certain," Edward said firmly. "You're not marrying anyone till you're very much better than you are now. Caroline, take her up to bed and give her one of the pills the doctor prescribed. At least it will give her a good night's sleep."

Meekly, keeping her confused thoughts to herself, she let herself be taken upstairs.

Paul phoned the next morning, as Edward was leaving for the office. Laura sat with hands tightly clenched, listening to the one-sided conversation.

"Didn't she? Well, there was no reason why she shouldn't have written from Italy, but frankly we've been very worried about her since she came home. . . . Yes. She's not at all well at the moment. . . . Could you?

Well, frankly, yes, I would. But, Paul, I think there's something you should know and it might make a difference. She told us last night she's going to marry Castleton. I'm sorry. . . . God knows. Will you? Tomorrow? It's very good of you. Yes, come straight round any time. Right, see you then."

Edward appeared at the dining-room door. "That was Paul, worried because you hadn't replied to his last two letters. He suddenly had the feeling last night that something was wrong and rang at the first opportunity. When he heard you weren't well, he said he'd come straight back instead of waiting till term starts next week."

Laura said flatly, "It's kind of him, but there's no need."

"And I might as well tell you," Edward went on heavily, "that I phoned Richard and Toby while you were out last night. They're both coming over tomorrow too."

"Isn't it gratifying, Laura," Caroline said caustically, "to have four strong men rushing to form a protective barrier round you? Anyone would think you were being forced to marry Lewis against your will!"

"You know quite well that this was arranged before we even heard about the proposed marriage," Edward said tiredly. "It's Laura's health that's our prime concern."

"Is Laura getting married?" Helen asked suddenly, surfacing from her comic. She wasn't usually allowed to read at table, but this morning she had taken advantage of her parents' obvious preoccupation.

"Yes," Laura answered in the same expressionless voice, "I'm going to marry Mr. Castleton."

"And Mummy and Daddy don't want you to?"

"Get on with your breakfast, Helen," Caroline said sharply.

Edward said awkwardly, "Laura, will you promise me

not to go out today? Not alone, anyway."

"All right." She wanted to comfort him, pitying his drawn face and anxious eyes, and in any case she felt tired and lethargic, totally unable to cope with the spinning universe that lay in wait for her beyond the walls of Four Winds. Edward and Richard, Toby and Paul, all of them ranged against Lewis and herself. Why? Had they any idea what was happening to her, or did they just instinctively sense danger?

"Phone if you need me, Caroline." Edward turned away and a moment later the front door closed behind him.

The next phone call, half an hour later, was from Lewis. "Darling, are they trying to put pressure on you?"

"All they've got!" she answered with grim humour. "There's to be a full-scale family conference at the weekend."

"Will there be any counsel for the defence?"

"I can manage," she said quietly.

"Noel, I can't see you today after all. I have to go up to Norfolk on one of these seaside assignments. The deadline's looming. I should have gone last week, but I didn't want to leave you just after you'd come back. The devil of it is I'll have to stay over the weekend. I was going to suggest you come with me, but in the circumstances you obviously can't. I'll ring you the minute I get back. Just hold on, darling. That's all you have to do."

Thoughtfully Laura replaced the receiver. She felt very, very tired and the prospect of three days without the strains and stresses of Lewis was undeniably comforting. Quite suddenly, the idea of the nursing home Dr. MacIntyre had mentioned took on the guise of a refuge rather than a prison. Just to be left in peace, to be able to rest—

234

After a moment she lifted the telephone again and began to dial.

It was a distressing weekend. Paul arrived soon after Richard and Toby on the Saturday afternoon. His hand gripped Laura's reassuringly, asking nothing, offering everything. She found she couldn't meet his eyes. When they were all seated solemnly in the sitting-room, she said hesitantly, "I rather fear you've all been brought here under false pretences. I told Edward last night that I'd asked Dr. MacIntyre to book me into Moorlands Nursing Home."

"What kind of a place is that?" Richard asked sharply.

"Psychiatric," answered Edward briefly, avoiding his eyes.

"He phoned me this morning," Laura went on. "I'm to go in on Monday. I think he rushed it through specially so I should be in before Lewis comes back from Norfolk."

Paul said in a low voice, "Do you really mean to marry him, Laura?"

"I rather think I have to."

Toby said violently, "Good God, girl, this is the twentieth century!"

"It has to be played out to the end."

They stared at her, their faces mirroring their individual unease. She turned to Caroline. "I know you haven't felt welcome in this house for some time and I'm sorry. It won't be for much longer."

"What the devil is she talking about?" Richard demanded hoarsely.

Caroline said rockily, "It's true, you know. There's been an awful feeling of resentment here for months. I don't know where it comes from, but I've hated it."

Edward reached out and drew her to his side.

Toby jumped to his feet. "Are we all going mad? For pity's sake, why didn't someone tell me what was going on? One thing's clear, at least. When she leaves the nursing home, she mustn't come back here. She can come to us, willingly, or go to Richard—"

"It's no good, Toby," Laura said gently. "I thought of that, too, when we came back from Italy, but I realized it wouldn't work. I'll never be free of Lewis now as long as he lives. Try to accept it. It won't be for much longer."

Caroline's trembling hands went to her mouth and it was left to Edward to say incredulously, "You mean— you *know* he—?"

Laura covered her face with her hands and began to sob hopelessly. They all made an instinctive movement to go to her, but it was Paul who reached her first. His arms went round her, oblivious of the rest of them.

"Hush, sweetheart, it's all right. If it won't be for long, at least that's something, and we must just hold on as best we can."

Edward repeated in a shaking voice, "You really believe she knows—?"

Paul held her closely against him. "Probably, she's known things before. Clairvoyance isn't unique, when all's said and done. The important thing is not to let it frighten her."

"Not frighten *her!*" muttered Toby under his breath. "It scares the pants off me!"

"What else has she known?"

Paul's eyes went up to Richard's steady, interrogative gaze. "I'm sorry; she made me promise not to repeat them."

"When was this?"

"Oh, months ago, when she first met Castleton." His face hardened. "My God, though, if I'd realized—"

"What is this hold he has over her?" Richard demanded.

"Don't blame Lewis," Laura said in a whisper. "He fought against it as hard as I did at first. He wouldn't accept it for a long time, until Noel—"

"Noel!" Paul and Caroline had spoken together and the others stared at them in surprise. Caroline flushed. "I believe that was the name of a girl Lewis was once in love with."

"Paul? You recognized the name too."

He hesitated and glanced at Laura. She gave an almost imperceptible nod and he said briefly, "Laura dreamt about Castleton a few days before she first met him. In the dream, he called her Noel."

"*Before* she met him?" Toby repeated.

Richard said gently, "What do you want us to do, Laurie? How can we best help you?"

She lifted her head suddenly. "She's coming back! I'm surprised she waited so long. Noel, just a moment— Oh, please!" Her voice rose despairingly and then a tremor passed over her and she freed herself from Paul's tightened hold.

"I really don't know what all the fuss is about," she said, and there was a faint but unmistakable American accent in her voice.

The silence which engulfed them was tangible, holding them fast in a total, horrified suspension of belief.

"Who are you?" Paul demanded urgently.

Her eyes rested on him with something like pity. "Paul, I'm sorry, really I am, but I did warn you. There can never be anyone but Lewis for me."

"And for Laura?" he whispered.

She opened her eyes very wide. "Why, Paul, I'm Laura!" she said, and as her eyes went round their frozen faces, she gave a low laugh of triumph.

EPILOGUE

Laura

Chapter 17

DURING the two weeks she spent at Moorlands, Noel, sensing danger, kept entirely away, and in her absence Laura slowly struggled through to a new understanding. It was very restful to lie back in the narrow bed and look up at the painted blue ceiling, letting the thoughts come and go in her head without worrying how they would seem to other people. The embryo of her love for Paul, free to grow unhampered for the first time, strengthened daily, but it wasn't until almost the end of her stay that she came to realize, with a dizzy sense of overwhelming relief, that in it lay her antidote to Noel. She had as much right as Noel to fight for a love of her own. At last they were on equal ground.

She tried to explain some of this to Edward on his visits. He listened gravely.

"You're quite sure you're free of her? Permanently, I mean?"

"Quite, quite sure. I don't know *how* I know, but I do. She'll never be able to come back again."

"Then this place really has helped you?"

"Oh, yes, Edward. It's such a wonderful relief to be able to stop fighting it, just to lie back and let it all come pouring out. The doctors and staff are wonderful, they never so much as raise an eyebrow. Of course, I've no idea what conclusions they're coming to about me, but I know in my own mind that the worst is over now. And Paul's letters are a great comfort. He writes every day, you know. The knowledge that he's waiting for me helps enormously."

"And what about Lewis? Have you thought what you're going to tell him?"

Her face clouded. "I've been trying not to think about that. The difficulty will be in trying to convince him that she really has gone for good. I haven't the strength to face him, Edward. I feel—drained, totally incapable of surviving anything that would involve any effort at all. In fact, I was going to ask if you'd mind if I went straight to Richard's when I leave here after all? Then I could write to Lewis from there and tell him the position. It will take time to live down all the associations Four Winds has had for me, and quite apart from that, I think Caroline deserves a rest. She's been under a strain too."

"Yes, apparently she was much more aware of what was going on than I was. I can't imagine why she didn't tell me, except—" He glanced across at her. "Well, you've probably realized, living in the same house, that Caro and I have been going through rather a difficult patch. It'll sort itself out, given time."

It was eventually arranged that Edward should collect her on the Saturday morning. Richard would drive down from London, have lunch with them all at Four Winds, and take her back with him. In that way they hoped to get her to London before Lewis learned of her leaving the nursing home. Paul would go straight to London and be waiting for her at Richard's flat rather than give rise to any suspicion by going to meet her at Four Winds. They would spend the Sunday together before he drove back in time for school on the Monday morning.

"What was the doctor's final verdict on me?" Laura en-

242

quired with interest as they drove out of the nursing home gates.

"A very cautious one, I felt. Jacobson made the point that if he'd merely read your case history, he would probably have been convinced that you were suffering from a paraphrenic illness such as schizophrenia. But having spoken to you, he's satisfied that your attitudes and responses are not those of someone who is mentally ill. All he would say was that your 'perceptions appear to be genuine' and that he believes you did actually hear and see what you said you did."

"Well, I suppose that's something."

"The fact remains, of course, that he can't explain *how*. We had a rather more general discussion on ESP and the psy factor and he quoted Isaac Newton and Lord knows who else. I can't say it was enlightening but it was certainly interesting."

Robert and Helen had returned to school while she was away and Peter was spending the day with some friends. Richard and Caroline came out to welcome her and they all went in together, but as Laura crossed the threshold, she was conscious of the house seeming to hold its breath. The drama wasn't quite over yet.

Over lunch the others chatted and laughed with the nervous gaiety that comes with relief from strain, but Laura, increasingly aware of some imminent danger, grew more and more silent. At last she pushed her plate away.

"I'm sorry. I'm too excited to eat. I'll just go up and put a few more things into the case I had with me at Moorlands. I can leave the rest here for now, can't I?"

"Of course," Caroline said brightly. "Would you like me to come and help you?"

"No, you finish your lunch. I won't be long." She picked up her handbag and walked as steadily as she could out of the security of the dining-room and stood for a moment looking up the wide staircase. What was it that was disturbing her so much? She was only aware of a tense, excited feeling of expectancy.

Step by step she went up the stairs, her heart thumping painfully. Would she ever be able to love this house of Edward's as it deserved to be loved, or had Noel's obsessive passion for it spoilt it for her for ever?

On the landing she paused again and listened. A burst of laughter reached her from the dining-room. In the kitchen, Mrs. Baines had her transistor blaring. Upstairs, all was quiet. It took a considerable effort to propel herself forward to her own room. She opened the door and waited. Everything was as it should be. She took a step inside and as she did so, a hand came over her mouth and Lewis's voice said in her ear, "It's all right, sweetheart. I'm sorry I had to frighten you. I wasn't sure who was coming."

She shook his hand away from her mouth and as she turned to look at him wild, unreasoning fear rushed over her. He was smiling down at her.

"You didn't really think I'd let them take you away a second time?"

She said numbly, "How—how did you—?"

"It was easy enough. Caroline had just taken young Peter off in the car. I simply walked up the drive and let myself in. Mrs. Baines was closeted in the kitchen and didn't hear a thing. I'd been watching the house for days, of course, and Peter's purposeful removal was the one hint I was waiting for. Look, darling, we'll have to hurry. I parked my car round the corner, down the side road.

We'll slip out through the French windows. They won't see us from the dining-room."

Her mouth was hot and dry, full of heartbeats. "Lewis—forgive me. I can't come with you."

"Of course you can. Give me your case and I'll help you pack. We haven't long. Caroline might come up to see how you're getting on."

"Lewis, I'm Laura!"

He paused to glance at her. "Yes, at the moment you are. It doesn't matter."

"I'll never be Noel again, Lewis."

He straightened slowly. "What did they do to you in that madhouse?"

"Just helped me to know myself better."

"They didn't hurt Noel?"

"Of course not. She wasn't there."

A frightened look crossed his face. "Laura, hurry—we must get away."

"I'm not coming, Lewis," she said as steadily as her tumultuous pulses would allow.

"Noel?" His eyes raked agonizingly over her face.

Wordlessly she shook her head.

"You *are* Noel!" His eyes focussed on her hair, soft round her face, and she saw his anguished doubt. If only one of them would come upstairs—if she could only find some way of attracting their attention—

"Come along, we're going!" His hand closed over her wrist but she twisted free, backing away from him, and in that moment, unbelievably, something appeared in his hand, something small and black and blunt and ugly. Her eyes dilated in horror, travelling slowly upwards from the weapon to his face. It was glistening with sweat, his face wide open and staring. He gave a low, excited laugh.

"It's all right, my darling. I shan't hurt you. I knew there was a chance that they wouldn't let you come. I came prepared."

"Lewis," she whispered frantically, backed up against the door. She was still clutching her handbag with both hands in an ineffectual attempt to shield herself from the menace that faced her, while her mind darted round the possibilities of wrenching open the door behind her. But it opened inwards, and before she could make more than one movement, he might—

He said rapidly, "This time, my darling, there will be no mistake. We really will go together and no one will ever separate us again."

She watched, completely paralyzed, as his hand came up.

"You won't feel a thing, my love."

She flung herself sideways a fraction too soon and his hand followed her unwaveringly. In a last, instinctive attempt to save herself, she again caught up the leather bag, holding it across her body with both hands, and in the same moment came the shattering jar of impact, all the more terrible for being almost silent. She hurtled backwards and the bag flew out of her hands. As she fell, she heard Lewis's cry—"Wait for me, Noel!" and another dull explosion as his body crashed to the floor.

There was a searing pain in her left arm and her ankle was twisted beneath her. It occurred to her slowly that she was capable of feeling pain, yet surely it wasn't possible that she was still alive? Cautiously she opened her eyes. Above her was the end of the bed, its flowered counterpane trailing on the carpet, and half under it lay the handbag, with a small, powder-scorched hole in the middle of it. She stared at it uncomprehendingly and as she did so a

246

coldness, tangible as the touch of a hand, brushed across her face in a gesture of farewell.

With an effort she raised her heavy, aching head, and quickly let it drop again. At her feet Lewis lay, still smiling, a neat hole in his right temple.

"Oh, God!" she whispered. "Oh, God!" How was it that he could possibly have missed her? Impossible that the soft leather of the bag could have deflected the bullet. She reached out a hand, stretching the fingers to the limit and inching her shoulder along the floor until she could touch the strap and draw it towards her.

Inside lay the bullet, harmless and spent beside the shattered silver compact. Noel—Lewis—Always. Tears of grief and weakness filled her eyes. So at the last Noel had saved her after all. She had no further need of her. She had Lewis, which was all she had ever wanted.

Downstairs, at last, a voice called her name, and footsteps came running up the stairs. With the mutilated compact tenderly cradled in her hand, she waited for the door to open.